Love Doesn't Work

Love Doesn't Work

seven dualist tales

Henning Koch

1334 Woodbourne Street
Westland, MI 48186
www.dzancbooks.org

"In Memoriam, Ingmar Bergman" was originally published in *Absinthe: New European Writing*, issue 9.

Published 2010 by Dzanc Books
Cover art: "Greta," by Cinzia Nieddu
Book design: Steven Seighman

06 07 08 09 10 11 5 4 3 2 1
First edition November 2010
ISBN-13: 978-0982520451

Printed in the United States of America

Contents

In Memoriam, Ingmar Bergman

Ingmar Bergman called me back after I left him a message about the flooded bathroom. I asked him to come at about three o'clock.

"How much do you charge per hour?" I said.

"175 crowns. Not too bad for a genius."

"I don't need a genius. I need a plumber."

"Don't you worry. I understand the realities of the situation better than most."

I didn't like employing Ingmar Bergmans for this kind of thing, but what the hell were you supposed to do? Normal plumbers cost a lot more, and since my retirement I had to think about such things. Also you got a bit of conversation out of it. Ingmar Bergmans liked to talk. I didn't speak Polish or Czech and I liked to hear a bit of Swedish now and then. Was that a crime?

He didn't arrive until twenty to four, and when he walked in he didn't even have the decency to apologize. Instead I got a moronic smile and an embarrassed shrug. "You know how it is," he said.

"I'm sorry to say I don't."

"Well you wouldn't, would you? You're not an artist."

He got started. It was a dirty job, a blocked exit pipe from the water closet, but he worked without complaint. I waited until he'd broken the hog's back, then asked him into the parlor for a cup of coffee.

"I don't really have time," he said, "but you want a chat, I suppose...?"

"Wash your hands please, Ingmar," I said.

Afterward, we sat on my late grandmother's best sofa with one of her lace tablecloths on the table, eating home-baked cinnamon buns baked to her recipe. Ingmar folded his hands in his lap.

"I guess you want to talk about film?" he said with disguised relish.

"What do you want to talk about?"

"Just because I'm an Ingmar Bergman doesn't mean we have to talk about film."

"But you're a genius film director. Everyone knows that."

"Listen to me," he said sharply. And then he went through everything I already knew.

In 2010 the Swedish Film Institute held a meeting to discuss the international crisis in Swedish film. There was no lack of directors in Sweden, but the quality was simply not there, just an endless parade of trendy young video dwarfs, beer-gutted monstrosities with plasticized wives, stuttering illiterates and self-glorifying mediocrity all over the place. Swedish films had begun to lose that ubiquitous Scandinavian feeling. Winter light. Snow glistening under the fir trees. A shoreline in Gotland where big waves roll in while a bearded man stands reflecting on his life in flashback. Norwegian fjord ponies with bells, burning torches on the sleighs, packs of wolves with lolling tongues, a peasant deflowering a goat in a byre, a girl with a basket picking blueberries in a dark forest, an old pastor in the sacristy snatching a quick glass of rye before Christmas Mass.

All this was on the verge of being lost forever.

Meanwhile, the people in the streets were ingesting hamburgers and flocking to see second-rate American films full of guns, drugs and decadent sex.

Men no longer said, "Miss Nyström looks very pretty today." They said, "Lena, you're looking horny. Fancy a tumble?"

And because of this the world had certainly become a worse place.

There was a stark realization at the Swedish Film Institute that radical measures were needed. Ingmar Bergman was called in, or rather, they grovelled and begged until given an audience at his home on Fårö.

Mr. Bergman was by then very advanced in years, tottering about with a stick. His mysterious eyes twinkled at the Film Institute Committee as he waited for them to speak. The Committee made a suggestion; Ingmar Bergman's face flushed with pride when he realized the implications. This was the masterstroke. His vision would dominate the Scandinavian millennium.

Slowly the words came stumbling over his dried lips: "I *am* Sweden."

And with this he allowed the doctors to take samples of his stem cells.

The Committee later brought these cells to Stockholm, where two hundred and fifty Ingmar Bergman clones were produced, then released like hungry lions among a herd of cud-chewing cattle.

Problems were evident almost from the very beginning.

The main problem, as the plumber suggested, was the diminutive size of the Swedish film industry. There wasn't room for two hundred and fifty geniuses on the playing field. A couple of Ingmar Bergmans ended up in California. One of them became a porn film director, but later shot himself. Another one set up a bakery and made large sums of money selling Swedish sweet buns stuffed with whipped cream and marzipan to the discerning customers of Beverly Hills. Later he was arrested for poisoning a number of celebrated network stars.

In Sweden, there was a bloodbath. Twenty-six Ingmar Bergmans disappeared. Several were found floating in the Baltic. One was later located in an ashram in Madhya Pradesh. A few ended up working in the Russian oil industry as drill platform operators, one was found cut into small pieces in a bin-liner in Malmö. Around fifty of the Ingmar Bergmans were detained in psychiatric hospitals, for which the government at once demanded compensation from the Swedish Film Institute. One Ingmar Bergman became the Chief Executive of the West Coast Fishermen's Federation, and disavowed any further interest in filmmaking.

Between those Ingmar Bergman clones that did venture into the film industry, there was internecine competition.

One Ingmar Bergman raised the necessary finance to make a film about a man involved in an extramarital affair with his own cousin. The set-up of the story was that the cousin had saved him from drowning when he was twelve years old. Ever after, the man lived with a terrible, phobic horror of water which made it difficult for him to take a shower. His wife—an evil, wart-speckled hag—hated him and refused even to sleep in the same room. Only his cousin could bring him out of these deep wells of panic and into the light. This lovely, suffering woman spent hours soothing him before he would enter the bathroom. Only with his cousin could he maintain his bodily hygiene while at the same time enjoying the fruits of a sexual relationship, albeit one that was considered taboo in society. His wife felt ill-used, maybe even justifiably so, yet this did not excuse her argumentative, angst-ridden behavior.

Two days before commencement of principal photography, Ingmar Bergman was run over by a tram.

Another Ingmar Bergman wanted to make a film about a woman who heard voices. Her psychologist was initially convinced that she was suffering from paranoid delusions, but in the course of their therapeutic sessions it gradually dawned on him that she was communing with his forefathers. Specifically, she was in contact with his ascetic great-great-grandfather, who repeatedly ordered him to stop working as a therapist and take up his true vocation as a wandering lay preacher.

This Ingmar Bergman was also killed, when a light plane flew into his house. The pilot was not an Ingmar Bergman, just an ordinary film director whose career lay in ruins.

One Ingmar Bergman stood out as a man of leadership, a quality the others lacked. He gathered a group of twenty Ingmar Bergmans around him, controlled their creative drives with a Proustian ferocity and forced them under oath and contract to work up his plot-lines into finished manuscripts. From time to time one of them disappeared, usually after creative differences or some brazen attempt to go ahead with a solo project.

The national media blustered and heckled about murder and corruption at the heart of Sweden's film industry, but its journalists were silenced with bribes or bullets. The Swedish film miracle was once again up-and-running, introducing the world to a new filmic genre, the so-called "death rattle," characterized by the presence of a dying person, usually a retired/semi-retired priest or schoolteacher reflecting on his/her life and reaching an insight that sparks a crisis. In many cases the resolution of this crisis hinges on the necessity of a reconciliation with a long-lost son/daughter. This long-lost person is travelling as fast as he/she can, in order to speak to the dying protagonist before he/she expires. Frequently this journey takes the form of a frantic chase on horseback—occasionally a sleigh with burning torches, occasionally a pack of wolves/bears/lynxes in pursuit, occasionally a blunderbuss used to dispatch a number of these wolves/bears/lynxes—through deep, almost impassable snow. On a couple of occasions, several Ingmar Bergmans used the device of an epic long-distance terrain-skating journey across a vast frozen lake inhabited by large, aggressive elk. In some cases this person, whether a friend/ex-lover/son/daughter, arrives too late to be enlightened by the last words muttered from the dying person's lips. In other cases, when the loved one does finally arrive, there is a further misunderstanding prompting the loved one to storm out of the house, leaving the dying person to bitterly contemplate an eternity of antagonism and unfulfilled love.

Audiences were thus obliged to endure the bittersweet reality of misinformed love, a truth destined never to be known outside the reality of the film. Ultimately the audience always turned round and looked at the cinema fire exits glowing in the dark, knowing they were now irretrievably lost, destined never again to enter the codex.

In fact, everywhere there were critics writing about Swedish cinema—"An almost Oriental purity of style and vision..." Or "Melodrama married through sparse visionary unity with the Japanese haiku form..."

Cinema audiences grew knowledgeable about every departure from the rules of the genre. There were sighs and irritated coughs every time a lesser Bergman attempted to innovate or depart from the established formats laid down by the greater Ingmar Bergmans.

For instance, one Ingmar Bergman, a member of the powerful "Script IB Group," tried to introduce a new dramaturgy in which a dying priest suddenly revives and establishes a loving relationship with his long-lost child.

Having thus displayed his poor judgment, this individual suddenly broke his sternum and was forced to retire from the film business.

After delivering his long-winded explanation, most of which I already knew and have more or less paraphrased here, Ingmar Bergman, my plumber, helped himself to a second cinnamon roll. Shaking with emotion, he chewed it intensely until it was a mere lump of dough in his throat, suitable only for swallowing and disposing of in the nether heartlands of his stomach, then his greater intestine.

I leaned forward and whispered: "If the chance presented itself, would you want to make a film of your own?"

Ingmar Bergman smiled coolly and focused his sad eyes on me. "My dear fellow, you must be utterly deranged! Do you really believe I would volunteer such information to you, a mere pensioner?"

Then it happened, that weird thing I am still sitting here wondering about. Should I have reported him to the Film Institute for recidivist behavior? After all, he had no license to indulge in creative activities.

Had I done so, I might have saved his life!

Ingmar Bergman got out a little camera and before I knew it, he had taken a photo of me.

Then he stood up and said, "I *always* photograph my clients. I'm assembling an enormous photo-collage composed of all these portraits."

"Whatever for?"

"If you stand at a good distance, you can see it's a self-portrait of me. I am using your identity to fashion a likeness of myself, because that is what we all do, my friend."

I was puzzled. Bergmans can be so puzzling. "So what's the meaning of it? This self-portrait?"

He smiled patiently. "If one has an ego, if one is a genius as I decidedly am, one has to do what one has to do. It has fallen to me to spend my life, indeed to waste my life, as a plumber. On the other hand I have no doubt that I would similarly feel I had squandered my years had I worked as a film director. All things are vain and meaningless except Art, and all attempts at making Art are doomed to fail."

"It makes me glad I'm not an artist myself."

"Indeed. Before I die I must have a finished portrait of myself, or my life will have been something worse than wasted. It will have been a lie!" He gestured dramatically in the air. "Ingmar Bergman, plumber! A simulacrum of my existence, made up of its constituents, the clients whose lives I have played a part in, whose pipes I have cut and soldered. Do you understand?"

"I have to confess, I don't."

"Ah well, how could you? You're not an Ingmar Bergman, as I am..."

With this, he stood up to leave. I paid him three hundred and fifty crowns in cash.

Soon after, I read in the newspaper that he had been gored to death by an elk whilst picking blueberries in Gotland, where he had gone to visit a dying relative and do a bit of skating. Remarkably, the police found no evidence of foul play in his death, although they did concede that the elk had misbehaved. The Swedish Film Institute issued a mendacious statement in which reference was made to his "honorable life spent faithfully serving as a member of the plumbing fraternity," while also calling attention to "the remarkable, visceral similarities in the manner of his passing to those depicted in countless numbers of Swedish films made by his beloved relatives."

I threw away the newspaper.

I am now waiting to die myself. I must confess, I am

sickened by the corruption of the world. How many hours, how many days have I sat here contemplating the meaning of Ingmar Bergman's life? Slowly, the dim, mysterious words he imparted to me have lost their veil. I have stepped into the clear light of his purpose. If only I could have seen his photo-collage. I might then have understood his need to express himself in sculpted light.

Yet any half-sane person would surely ask himself why a photo-collage should be so important? Why does it really matter?

Two months after the news of his death, the toilet was blocked once again.

This time I paid for a proper plumber, who arrived on time. Unlike my Bergman, he didn't have time for coffee. As soon as he'd sorted out the problem, he muttered some sort of goodbye in a heavy accent, and left without another word.

I stood in the window and watched him pack his tools into the back of his van. It occurred to me that, in one sense, he was an even greater mystery than Ingmar Bergman. There are people in this world who do not say very much, who have no avowed purpose other than putting bread on the table as efficiently as possible.

Had I been born an Ingmar Bergman I would have made a film about *them*.

A Mad World, Mister

I

Harold was a young Stockholmer whose life from the outside seemed poised for happiness. There was one problem, however, which he did his best never to discuss with anyone. In a nutshell, he was claustrophobic.

Wherever he lived, however spacious his apartment, it always struck him as slightly cramped. Sometimes he paced through his rooms dreaming of *space*, apparently the one thing he did not and could not have.

Often he played a little mental game, which involved him looking at, for instance, the living room whilst thinking to himself: "If this were twice as big, would I make it into two separate rooms? Or just have a bigger living room?"

He saw before him a billiard table, a highly polished glass

drinks cabinet, and wall-to-wall built-in bookcases equipped with an old-fashioned ladder running smoothly along a runner set into the floor.

Then he saw himself, standing by the billiard table with a cigar in one hand, a glass of whisky in the other, a moustache like a black caterpillar crawling under his nose, and a beautiful, spirited *Cubana* in his arms, laughing infectiously as she kissed him, her sharp-heeled shoes drumming restlessly against the parquet.

What an overflowing cup of humanity he would have at his billiards evenings! Poets, philosophers, actors and ballet dancers, explorers, geneticists, maybe even the odd normal person, who would find himself in a minority, the toast of all and a great object of curiosity.

In real life Harold was a conscientious man who worked hard and kept his overcoat dry-cleaned and his shoes well polished at all times. Above all he had his positive-minded, capable Linda. They'd been living together for two years; it had worked well because Linda really was *linda,* as they say in Spain. She never failed to snuggle up to him and smother him in kisses. At the same time she was a sensible woman who brought home a salary and always made sure the bills were paid on time.

In spite of her good qualities, Harold never seemed to pluck up the courage to ask her to marry him. Occasionally when she was out he'd practice his marriage proposal in the bathroom mirror, but he was never quite convinced by his own performance.

Everything was fine in Harold and Linda's world, except for this contentious issue of space—because, at the end of each menstrual cycle, Linda became depressed at the thought of her unborn children.

Every month a child died inside her, leaving a void.

October came round again and she had her thirty-seventh birthday. They went out for a Chinese meal with friends. It was a success. They talked about property, future movements in property prices, whether to buy or rent. One woman had thought it better to rent, a man had disagreed with her. Then the subject of Europe came up. Someone advocated that Sweden should join the foreign exchange mechanism. Someone else insisted it should not.

Harold had concentrated on making the duck pancake rolls and occasionally offering one to Linda. On the way home, Linda grabbed his arm, squeezed it and said, "Harold? Why do you never say anything? When we're with people."

He thought about it. "It's because everyone else is so busy talking. And I'm not sure they really want me to interrupt."

"But that's not the actual reason, is it?"

"No," said Harold. "To be honest, I don't really care about those things. Property, Europe..."

"Aren't you at all interested? I mean we have a property and we live in a country in the European Community."

"Do you mind if I'm honest? Those things bore me rigid."

"What do you want to talk about, then?"

They walked home in silence.

He woke up abruptly in the night. Linda was sitting up in the bed like a little owl, gazing at the duvet with her sharp nose in profile.

He was unnerved. "What is it darling? Have you got a stomach ache? Can I make you some camomile tea?"

"I don't have a stomach ache."

"Oh, isn't it that time of the month?"

"I want a child," she said. Her words filled the room and rumbled against the walls, even rattling the front door slightly.

Harold wound up his thoughts, then mechanically released them. "Anyone can have a child," he began. "But a happy child, that's a rarity. A happy child with two happy parents, that's almost unheard of. The world is a harsh place. Maybe it's better to leave the children where they are, in the unexpressed world where they're blissfully unaware of ever having lived at all. Where no human ties or disappointments or pain will ever plague them. Anyway, we don't have much space in this flat."

"I can feel my children inside me. They're knocking against my insides and they want to come out. Harold, why can't you just oblige me?" she whispered. "Take off your pajamas and put away your condoms. Come inside me every night. Enjoy yourself."

The idea was appealing, but Harold felt worried by her insistence.

Winter started creeping in, unwelcome as always. People put on their frowns before they went out. It was also a cool period in Harold and Linda's relationship.

When they set off for work in the mornings, they rarely stopped off at the café to have a cappuccino together like they used to. It was a relief to perform only a cursory muzzling of their lips, then murmur a quick goodbye and walk on in blessed solitude.

In spite of always trying to do what one should, Harold was not a popular person. Many of their friends actually disliked him, and had made it clear to Linda that she should leave him before it was too late. Harold couldn't understand why people didn't like him. Old ladies smiled at him pleasantly enough as he walked down the pavement, but men and women of his own age frowned and looked away.

Was there anything wrong with being a well manicured, carefully presented clean-shaven young banker with fur-lined kidskin gloves, a leather briefcase and a cashmere overcoat? Was there anything contemptible about listening to what people said, agreeing affably whenever it was possible to do so?

II

The day after Linda's birthday, as he was making his way to the office, Harold experienced something very unsettling. At first he put it down to too many whisky sours the night before, but there it was: the world was moving, very slightly, all round him. To be specific, it wasn't so much the world as a section of the pavement on the corner of Nytorgsgatan. When he tried his foot against the paving stones they were springy like the mossy surface of a bog.

He stood, irresolute for a while, watching as other hurried walkers crossed the flexing section of the pavement. None of them noticed. In fact, several of them were more concerned about the spectacle of Harold standing there glaring at the ground, and occasionally kicking it with his highly polished brogues.

The bells of St. Maria struck eight-thirty and Harold moved on.

In the evening when Harold returned he'd bought a steel-tipped umbrella, which he dug into the tarmac by a lamp post. Soon enough he'd made a little hole, knelt down and poked his finger through. He got down on his knees and peered into the hole. Nothing. Just black. An odd smell came up through the hole. Was it sulphur? Or some sort of natural gas? He straightened up. What was needed here was a torch and a plumb line.

Back home, Linda was curled up in the sofa watching a DVD on how to improve your diet and fitness for pregnancy, while at the same time lacquering her toenails, as if intentionally ignoring the fact that Harold was slightly phobic about lacquered toenails, which made him wince.

Harold had the uncomfortable feeling that he was not a man at all and felt himself retreating through puberty into boyhood. His voice grew high-pitched in his throat, and his limbs lost their hair, once again acquired a chubby softness.

"Darling," he squeaked.

"What?"

"Why are you so angry with me? What have I done?"

"Harold. You have done nothing. You have never done anything." She turned her face to him, and he was astonished that she had also receded into childhood. Her hair hung down in damp ringlets. She wore a soft yellow towelling robe which scarcely reached down to her knees and she'd tucked her favorite doll under her arm. "By the way, I just had a shower," she said. "I am very clean."

"I can see that."

"If you want a shower too, that might be nice. There's nothing worse than a dirty man."

"You used to say you loved my smell," said Harold.

"Yes but that was just after I met you. I was still at the stage of trying to brainwash myself that you were perfect. Now I know you're not."

Harold put down his briefcase, relieved that she was talking to him at least. "How can you say I've never done anything?"

"Because you haven't. When I think of your life, I think of a big yawning emptiness."

Harold closed the front door and went into the kitchen without another word. He put on the coffee and sat in the window seat to read the newspaper. It was full of a repetitious banality that almost made him feel sick. The only headline he inadvertently caught before folding it up and hiding it under the table was "Man Eaten by Cat." He considered what it would be like being eaten by a cat. Surely one would have to actually want to be eaten? Only a debilitated, possibly comatose person would lie still long enough for its tiny jaws to inflict mortal wounds. That must be the answer. The man had a stroke and, after a few days of lying motionless on the floor, the cat started eating him.

The coffee pot was bubbling and Harold quickly turned it off to avoid any bitter aftertaste. While the milk was heating up he took the newspaper and went to the ceramic-tiled fireplace in the corner of the living room. He opened the little brass doors, stuffed the newspaper inside, then put a match to it.

Linda smelt the smoke. "What are you doing?" she called out.

"I'm burning the newspaper."

"Why? I haven't read it yet."

"Don't."

Linda stood in the doorway, looking at him strangely. "Why shouldn't I read the newspaper?"

"Newspapers create an image of life that's not only false but evil," said Harold. "They waste our time; stop us from thinking; lull us into a false sense of security."

He went back into the kitchen, boiled the milk and poured himself a nice café latte. "Do you want coffee?" he called out.

"I'm not drinking coffee."

"Why not?"

"It makes you less fertile."

Oddly enough, sitting there looking out of the window at the bored people walking along the river with their dogs, stopping to say hello to other bored people, fumbling for something to say, he wanted nothing but to open the now-burnt newspaper and sit there with his coffee, reading a pack of lies about how all this was normal.

Linda walked into the kitchen. "Are you having a bath?"

"No. I'm tired."

"I'm going to bed," she said.

Harold looked at the kitchen clock and realized with a shock that it was ten-thirty at night. It had taken him four hours to get home from work and have a cup of coffee.

III

The next morning, Harold woke up with a sense of purpose. Linda lay demonstratively with her back to him even though she was awake. He ignored her, got up, showered, shaved; then after breakfasting on yogurt, sliced apple, pumpernickel bread with hard Austrian cheese and pickled gherkins, he brought Linda breakfast in bed on the pretty, floral-patterned tray they had bought in Florence.

He knew what she liked when she was down: a slice of cake, a cup of herbal tea and a lit candle.

He sat by her side for a while. She tried not to show that she was pleased.

"Aren't you going to work?" he said.

"I've got a pain," she said. "In my stomach. I think I better stay at home, rest a bit. What about you? You're going to be late."

"I'm taking the day off. Going fishing."

"You never take a day off work, Harold. You never go fishing."

"I'm not really going fishing."

She munched her cake and looked at him. "Would you mind telling me what's going on? In your head, I mean?"

"Linda, I don't know quite how to put this, but... I've found a hole in the pavement and it's really bothering me. I think someone could fall into it."

"I didn't know you were so interested in road works."

"It's nothing to joke about, Linda. It's a deep hole, incredibly deep. It could be lethal."

"For God's sake! Don't you have more important things to worry about?"

He stood up. "I'm going to find out how deep it is, then report it to the City Council. I have to be responsible. If I don't do this, someone could get hurt."

"I'm the one who's hurt, Harold. I'm very hurt."

"At least you haven't fallen down a hole," said Harold, standing up and giving her a quick peck on the cheek before slipping out.

In the hall, he took his telescopic fishing rod, the fishing reel and the small box of tackle. He stood staring at his coats for a good long while, trying to decide whether to put on his usual cashmere overcoat or opt for his leather pilot jacket. Linda came out into the hall and walked into the bathroom. The door slammed behind her.

Harold took a deep breath, snatched the pilot jacket off its hanger and walked out. Just to reciprocate, he also slammed the door.

IV

Harold had not seen Stockholm mid-morning on a weekday since his undergraduate days more than five years ago. Everywhere there were people with time on their hands. Some also had money, which struck him as anomalous. Women shopping. Young men browsing in music shops. Why weren't they at work?

Strolling down the familiar streets, he felt ashamed of himself. Here he was, a man in the middle of his career, with a fishing rod in his hand. If anyone from the office should see him now, it would certainly not look good. He pulled up the collar of his leather jacket and sneaked along the back streets.

When he reached the hole, he saw it had enlarged enough for him to peer down and see its rocky sides widening as they descended into pitch black. He took his fishing rod out of its case and extended it to its full length.

The reel sang. At 150 meters his line ran out, but he had still not touched bottom.

Troubled, he looked up. Linda was standing on the street corner, looking at him. Quite a few other people had stopped and were giving him the once over. Quickly he started reeling in his line. When he looked up again, Linda was standing right next to him.

"Harold. What's going on?" she said.

He almost broke into a sweat getting the last of the line in, then packed his rod away and straightened up. "You know what I'm doing. I told you this morning. I'm trying to measure the depth of this bloody hole. Okay?"

"Okay." Her eyes grew moist as they always did when she got emotional about something. She reached out and caressed his cheek, then left without another word.

Harold spent the rest of the morning pacing round streets in the locality, examining the tarmac for that same spongy feeling as on the corner of Nytorgsgatan. It was all solid except in one spot, where extensive cracking seemed to indicate the formation of a large hole under the pavement. This cavity might conceivably be part of the same structure, although, of course, a hole does not have any structure except the gaseous molecules inside it.

In an infinity of space, would there still be a claustrophobia in one's body, a claustrophobia of suspension? He pondered this while he ate a shish kebab, sitting on a low wall with his fishing rod case leaning up next to him.

Then, when heading homewards, he saw a truly shocking thing.

As he came round the corner of Nytorgsgatan, an old lady fell through the pavement by the lamp-post. She fell like a stone, without a sound. Even her wheeled shopping trolley went in after her, like an articulated lorry tumbling over the edge of a precipice.

Harold ran up to the hole, which was now the width of a toilet-lid, just about enough for a skinny lady to go through. He put his head down the hole and stared down.

"Hello!" he shouted.

No one made any reply from the depths. He shouted again, even though he knew instinctively it was useless. She was already dead or dying.

Immediately he called up the City Council to report the hole and explain that he'd seen someone falling into it.

Within an hour they had sent a van, and set up a cordon preventing pedestrians from walking along the pavement. A small sign politely requested they cross the street and walk on the other side.

Harold was in deep shock. He approached one of the burly road-workers who had spilled out of the van to let him know about the old lady.

"You'll have to have a word with the emergency services about that," said the road-worker. "We're checking the pavement, but there's nothing here worth getting stewed up about. Just a little crack in the tarmac." He had an amused look on his face. His lips bulged, his mouth was so stuffed with snuff he could scarcely talk and his furry brown arms were covered in tattoos. Harold sighed. Clearly, he would have to speak to someone more senior.

As soon as he walked into the flat he knew that Linda was not there. Admittedly this was not so difficult to gauge, given that she had removed her coats from the coat-rack. Other things she had taken included CDs, DVDs, toiletries, books, a laptop and all of her clothes from the wardrobe. The place looked bigger, somehow.

In the bed, right in the middle, she had very pointedly left her doll.

On the kitchen table was a note, which he distractedly looked at, deciding to read it later once he had made his phone call to the City Council.

On the fridge was another note, held in place by a fridge magnet. It said: "Check the freezer. I have frozen ten portions of beef stroganoff." He wondered if this meant she would be back in ten days.

He went into the living room and, after consulting the telephone directory, put a call through to the Manager of Roads, Footpaths, and Cycle Lanes at the City Council. Unfortunately, the manager was not at his desk. According to his secretary, he was at an urban regeneration conference in Kuala Lumpur. Still, the secretary, who seemed fairly capable and senior, was willing to discuss Harold's urgent matter.

Harold quickly and efficiently summarized what he had seen, that is, the old lady falling down a hole in the pavement.

The secretary was quiet, and then she said: "Was an ambulance called?"

"No. The council workers showed up and they said there wasn't a hole."

"If there wasn't a hole then how do you suppose a woman fell into it?" she said. Harold could almost visualize her glancing at her watch.

"Can I be frank? This is a very deep hole, I suspect what we're dealing with here is a displacement of the earth's crust."

There was a loud sigh. "Oh Christ."

"I know. It's serious. Look, I'm not a deluded person. I'm a banker. I've taken the day off just to examine this hole. It's at least 150 meters deep, and my own personal feeling is it's a hell of a lot deeper than that."

The telephone made a click.

Harold stared at the phone for a while, then called the emergency services. A curt, anonymous voice answered.

"Your name?"

"Yes, I'd like to report a person falling into a hole in the pavement," said Harold.

"Your name, sir."

"Harold Blomkvist."

"Can you give me a location?"

"Absolutely. It's on the corner of Nytorgsgatan, Södermalm."

"Any idea of the victim's injuries?"

"I would have thought she's dead but I'm not sure."

After a few more routine questions, the operator hung up. Harold quickly put on his coat again and ran down to the corner of Nytorgsgatan. The ambulance and police car were already there with their blue lights flashing. Some ambulance personnel were searching the scene, presumably puzzled to find neither a hole nor anyone lying injured at the bottom of it.

Harold stepped forward to explain. A few minutes later he was sitting in the police car with a frowning constable.

"You're not listening to me," said Harold. "A woman died here today when she fell through."

"I'm sorry, we prosecute when members of the general public call us out maliciously and waste valuable time better spent helping genuine victims."

"Do I look like a madman?"

"Who knows? Madmen come in all shapes and sizes."

"I saw what I saw."

"You have nothing to back you up. And there are no old ladies missing anywhere. That thing you saw falling into this supposed hole of yours was not an old lady at all..."

"Fine. If it wasn't an old lady, what was it then?"

"It could have been anything. A black bin liner blown along by the wind?"

"This was no bin liner."

The policeman smiled. His teeth and gums looked like small pieces of yellow cheese stuck into regurgitated bacon rind. Harold tried to keep his composure. He hated poor hygiene more than anything.

"Anyone can make a mistake," said the constable. "It happens. We'll let you off this time, but we've got your name and address. If you call us out again you'll be prosecuted without fail."

That evening, Harold was in a somber mood as he ate his beef stroganoff.

First there was the matter of Linda. Her absence was making him uneasy. The flat was never silent like this. Even when he strained his ears, all he could hear was a high-pitched whine of air. Or maybe it was just his ears malfunctioning?

Occasionally a car went past or a plane flew over. It occurred to him that people everywhere were equating movement with some sort of meaning. The whole thing had kicked off with Magellan, Marco Polo, Columbus. Whenever people traveled somewhere, they felt their lives were significant. Even if they just drove somewhere, they had done something. In fact all they had done was to shift their carcasses somewhere else. Who cared if some fool sat at a café table in Venice looking at a pizza, or at a café table in Dresden looking at a Bratwurst?

As for Linda, did it matter that she had gone? If he were up there in space looking down at the planet, would he be able to say, "Ah, there's the place where a woman named Linda cohabits with Harold, although she seems to have temporarily moved out" Or would that be an irrelevance when juxtaposed with interesting enormities like the Great Wall of China?

Yes, this was the real question.

Suddenly it occurred to Harold that he needed someone to say, "Harold, you are a very confused man." The trouble was, he had no one to enunciate those words. Instead he was left with a problem.

He had discovered a huge and growing hole under his city. Soon they would all fall into this hole. They would fall for an eternity. They would not die when they hit the bottom, or by dashing themselves against the rock walls. They would fall forever. They would die of starvation, of boredom.

Even though he was exhausted, Harold put on his leather jacket and went out again for another peek at the hole. It was refreshing to walk under the open, arching sky, now liberally speckled with stars.

The pavement had been patched up, and when he walked across it, it seemed more solid. Even when he put all of his weight on it, he didn't feel it moving.

He panicked. What if it had all been a terrible mistake? What if the world were not coming to an end?

As he walked home, there was something bothering him.

Only when he slotted the front door key into the lock and opened the door did he realize what it was. Today was the second day he had not gone to work. He had not informed the Personnel Director. Tomorrow he would have to call in and explain that he was having a problem, a very real problem.

He could already read the mind of his Personnel Director: "Can't say I'm surprised he's had a collapse. He's so damned normal it's abnormal; no one will even sit next to him in the canteen, just talking to him drives people round the bend."

And what would he say?

Would he say, "There are some issues in my current life that are incompatible with normal work routines"?

Yes, that is what he'd say when he called in.

The bank would pay for therapy, he'd spend a few months on sick leave and then he'd go back to the office. His colleagues would all whisper about him but he'd be forgiven.

A nervous breakdown must be exactly like this. One saw reality for a moment. Then it became unmanageable. Like a huge balloon rising up before one, it ripped and collapsed. With a shock one realized it had nothing inside except for air. It was an illusion of solidity, nothing else.

V

Before he went to bed, he remembered the note on the kitchen table. All it said was that he must get some help. Then a telephone number of a therapist, and the time of his first appointment, which Linda had already set up for him.

That night, Harold had disturbing dreams.

He dreamt that he woke up in the middle of the night, then got dressed and went outside. Linda was standing in the sodium glare of a streetlight. Her lips were encrusted with small, sharp diamonds. When he kissed her mouth it was like kissing a brooch with a soft tongue lurking in its hard crack. Her hair was gilded and hung stiffly down like a glittering helmet, the decorated head of an Egyptian mummy.

"Why did you come back?" Harold asked.

"I couldn't leave. We're prisoners," she said. "Look!"

He turned his head and registered the fact that they were in a cell, the sort of cell one used to see in American Westerns. There was even a sheriff on the other side of the bars, tipping his chair and watching Harold and Linda with dull interest as he chewed his toothpick.

Linda sank down into the snow, and Harold positioned

himself behind her, spreading his legs so she could lean back against his chest. The flimsy gauze of her dress rubbed against him, and he grew powerfully tumescent. Linda seemed pleased. She looked back at him and smiled; then started dealing some cards, which weren't cards at all, but large moths gently flexing their patterned wings. Occasionally one of the moths tired of the proceedings and fluttered away, leaving them short-handed.

Next, Harold and Linda were teleported to the corner of Nytorgsgatan. Two police officers in a parked Volvo were keeping an eye on the hole. One of them opened a thermos and poured himself a cup of thick pea soup.

After a while they turned on their flashing lights and drove off.

Harold and Linda moved closer to the gaping hole.

"Why are we here again?" she said. "What can we do, Harold?"

"Don't you understand, Linda? This whole city is going to disappear. All our friends, every person living here is blissfully unaware of the fact that there's a yawning gulf just below their feet. We have to call someone."

"All right. Tell me who, then?"

"I don't know."

They stood in silence. The icy wind assaulted them, like a blast from infinity.

Next, Harold was watching a televised image of a landing strip at an airport, with a monstrous jet plane looming just above it, its wheels touching the tarmac with a little puff of smoke. Without an explosion, acrid smoke or flames, even without a sound, the runway ripped like a huge piece of paper and the plane disappeared. The police were quickly on the scene. A tarpaulin the size of a football pitch was stretched across the runway. Witnesses were rounded up and taken away in coaches.

The evening news bulletin reported that a group of anarchists had tried to dupe the general public with a cowardly trick. The airline had sent its spokesman to the news studio.

"There's been no loss of planes, so it seems rather redundant to speak of an air disaster, wouldn't you agree?" said the spokesman. "We are living in a world that is being taken over by terrorists and other elements actively working against democracy, equality, and other civilized values."

A few moments later the Prime Minister appeared to make a statement. It ran from his mouth like gravy: "We are talking of a plane that does not exist, hundreds of witnesses that do not exist, a hundred and fifty passengers that no one has managed to name. In other words, we are talking of a staged, simulated event, a trick organized by a group of a highly motivated and dangerous individuals, all of whom will be hunted down, arrested and punished vigorously through our legal system."

That same night, Harold and Linda packed clothes and food in a rucksack and took the back door out of the apartment block, exiting via the stinking refuse room in the basement.

Two hours later a group of plain-clothes police officers arrived, kicked in the door and submitted the whole flat to a careful search, even ripped the sofa apart and took up the floorboards and looked in suitcases for secret compartments.

When they found nothing, they concluded that Harold and Linda were part of a terrorist cell.

Having spent his whole life longing for more space, Harold now found himself living under the open sky among a group of people who'd taken refuge in the Greenstone Mountains of Västerbotten, close to the Arctic Circle.

A geologist from Uppsala University had advised them that the earth's crust was older and deeper here. Here, if anywhere, they would have firm ground under their feet until the end of time.

Behind them, Stockholm had already collapsed into the abyss.

Linda was a changed woman. She was tougher and more resourceful, always sewing or making ingenious devices for cooking over open fires, with a train of children behind her, always one at her breast and several more hanging at her skirts.

Harold had to admit that their children were very lovable. As for Linda, now that she had her children she seemed less concerned about Harold. He was a spent force, a cracked amphora whose value had been proved, although lately eclipsed by these small growing entities whose significance was infinite and almost cosmic.

Sometimes Harold reflected that he would never again walk along city streets, browsing for CDs or renewing his insurance policy at the broker's. Such things were now obsolete. Along with everything else, they had gone down the hole.

One day a fleet of military helicopters arrived, landing on a piece of level ground and disgorging a number of Ministers and high public officials with their assorted wives, husbands and families. The politicians did not speak to the settlers, merely threw embarrassed glances in their direction. In no time at all they had built a palisade and, within it, a village of strong, timbered houses with proper stone chimneys. Guards were placed at the gates.

The government announced a public meeting, at which the Prime Minister set about justifying his policies. As soon as the Cabinet had found out about the hole, he explained, it was thought more merciful to keep the truth from the people. This was partly to avoid panic. After all, the entire population could not have emigrated to the mountaintops of Västerbotten.

The Prime Minister also reported that all the major cities of the world had fallen into the bottomless void. Who knew where the Eiffel Tower was now, or Big Ben?

Maybe one day the planet would spew forth lava and build new continents. When this happened, the human race would come down from the mountains and build a new Jerusalem based on the same Grecian ideals.

The years passed. Disease and starvation were widespread among the settlers. The bureaucrats, with their solid houses and well-stocked warehouses behind the palisade, had an abundance of food and medicine. Occasionally they would make a grand gesture and donate some medicine to a dying settler outside the walls.

Sometimes at night Harold could hear the politicians standing on prominent rocks, practicing the speeches they would make on the day the first foundation stone was laid for the reconstruction of Stockholm.

VI

He woke from the dream at three in the morning. Outside, a storm was hammering the building. The gods were angry.

Harold looked for Linda but she was not in the bed and not in the bathroom either. Then he remembered that she had gone. Probably she was staying with her sister in Solna, but he knew he mustn't telephone her there, or ask her to come home. Linda was not like that. Leaving, for her, had been a final gesture. Harold closed his eyes and tried not to cry. Things snapped sharply into focus, like new-broken glass.

At first he had an absurd vision: he saw the lady with the shopping trolley, falling through the air and occasionally making a slow revolution. In her hand she held an umbrella, like a sort of Mary Poppins figure in a neatly buttoned blue overcoat, her hair held in place by a hat and hat-pins. She still had not reached the bottom of the hole! Her eyes were wide-open, more in amazement than terror.

Then, as he moved in closer, he recognized Linda's features, so familiar yet out of reach.

Even as she fell, she grew aware of him and looked over with a hurt, disappointed expression. There was a finality there, a realization that nothing could be changed.

Harold understood that he had created the bottomless hole, and now his Linda would be falling forever.

Love Doesn't Work

I

My world is limitation, has been limitation from beginning to end. I've gotten used to it. The first time I saw a woman naked I looked at her and thought, "My God, it's not what I thought!" And when I went to the obligatory places for the first time—Venice, Paris, Barcelona—they struck me as self-conscious arenas designed for the tourist to come and buy a postcard. Consumed, empty theatres.

At any rate, when I woke in the morning in my friend's house, I wasn't prepared for the utter brilliance of it all. He had bought acres of derelict houses in a tumbledown medieval town in Sardinia, then somehow managed to persuade the authorities to let him knock them all together and build a big white pod that dwarfed everything else in the town.

All his architectural ideas were invested in that building. There were stark concrete terraces with overhanging Tibetan eaves and carved dragon's heads; arrangements of terracotta pots with flowering plants; teak decking; plunge pools of fragrant juniper wood imported from Finland; a library with built-in bookcases; a secret door to the music room; a snooker room where the green baize of the table was always brushed, the symmetrical polished balls pristine as a Derbyshire tea-set; overlooked by a donnish bar stocked with every conceivable malt whisky, behind it a vulgar touristic map in the background, framed in dark wood, displaying "The Great Whiskies of the Auld Country."

"How the heck did you get planning permission for this?" I asked him, and he laughed with that anything-can-be-done expression of the land of his birth, California.

"Never ever ask an architect how he swung the fucking planning application," he oozed, almost breaking into an oily sweat at the thought of his triumph. "If against your better judgment you do ask, don't have any illusions about getting the truth, because you won't get it." Before I could respond, he added: "You know, sometimes decay works in your favor. I told them this street would fall down if nothing was done. My builders saved fifteen houses adjoining this building."

"So that's the truth, then?"

"Plus I offered an anonymous donation to the municipality."

"If you have money there are no problems, only solutions."

There was something petulant in my voice when I said that. I was a penniless Londoner, flown in to visit my big-shot friend. He had always approved of me, said I was a "genuine phoney," a phrase he stole from *Breakfast at Tiffany's.* He's not concerned with originality, he's a straight-talking Jimmy from Sacramento and nothing ever went wrong in his life.

"That's not quite true. Money is simplistic, kind of like a lens. If you have money you're looking through one lens, and if you don't you're looking through another. But neither is true."

"That's profound, Jimmy. Profound. But I still don't understand what the hell possessed you to live here. What do you do here? Don't you get bored?"

"Bored? Sure I get bored. I get bored anywhere, Chuck. Boredom ..." he muttered, frowning as his sluggish brain-cells dug into the problem, "...is the human condition. That's why I'm into form, and structure, and startling buildings. We need all that, we need beauty, Chuck. Or we're fucking finished."

We were sitting on a terrace outside his library, an incredible number of swifts and swallows darting over the tiled roofs below us, screaming as they tumbled with great daring through the air. To make things even more scenic, we were drinking green tea out of Chinese hand-bowls. People like Jimmy always employ interior decorators with an ill-disguised hostility towards handles, even door handles... in fact doors altogether are anathema to an architect worth his salt. In design-land, every room has to be open-plan, every little object has to scream out its identity and, above all, the identity of its owner.

There was something bemused about the way Jimmy acceded to design. I genuinely believe he had no aesthetics of his own. He had simply decided to be successful, and after that he'd aped what he saw in magazines, or in his friends. As we stood there talking, I considered the absurdity of a large, fluorescently yellow pig placed daringly against the window. Its bulky balls suggested the message of the piece, something like, "Hey, I'm ugly but I'm full of spunk." I thought of Jimmy getting up in the morning, calling out to his latest girlfriend before he gets into his station wagon to drive into Los Angeles: "There's something I gotta do, honey. Gotta get myself that pig, remember the one we saw yesterday? I couldn't sleep all night, it would just look great in Sardinia. You know my friend Dennis? He's invested in a Perspex calf. I reckon plastic animals are kind of zeitgeist. Soon they'll all be extinct and we're gonna be like that old Indian chief said. Dying of loneliness."

Jimmy. Always talking about zeitgeist. That bullshit word. *Zeitgeist, leitmotif, Forbes Magazine.* These were the Holy Trinity.

Everything had been fine for Jimmy until one day he decided a man of substance must have a wife. That was when his problems started.

A wife presented some major disadvantages. A knock-out wife could not be bought or downloaded. Even Jimmy, with his clueless, status-obsessed mind and his concern for the outward appearances of everything, knew that wife acquisition, at its most fundamental, was about what you had to offer inside. You could buff up your inner spirit, pay for a hell of a lot of therapy and spend a substantial amount of time meditating in Himachal Pradesh, but if you were still the sort of person who loathed sharing a toothbrush with your lover, it was unlikely that you would ever make her happy.

Most women, Jimmy had confided in me once, are too into intimacy.

"So beauty, Jimmy. Very big word, that. You think you found it?"

"You dumb shit. You can't find beauty. You can only be a seeker," said Jimmy, with a slight flickering of the eyes, signifying he didn't know what he was talking about.

"Where did you read that?"

"Oh, in some book." He waddled over to the bar, where he took a few cut-glass tumblers from a cabinet, dropped in some ice cubes and filled them with single malt.

"Speaking of beauty, when am I going to meet your wife?"

"Now you're making assumptions."

"Well they're usually beautiful, your women. I'd be bloody impressed if you ever fell for a normal-looking type your own age. I suppose you come down here for the good life? Eat well, go swimming, have a game of tennis in the morning, all that?"

"We don't live here. I would never live in south-east Sardinia, for Christ's sake, that would be the end of my career," said Jimmy.

"I do get bored here, but it's good to be bored sometimes. My brain needs a rest sometimes. I work hard, you know. I even work when I'm sleeping. A good architect has to give people what they want before they know they want it."

"And your wife likes it here?"

"Why do you have to bring up my wife all the time?"

"I'm curious, for God's sake. You're so mysterious about her. And it's all so recent."

"Not really. I ran into her about six months ago. Took her for dinner a few times, and then we went to Aspen, hung out, had a few steam-baths."

"That's what I mean. One minute you're a normal thrusting architect building up your firm in Manhattan and doing very nicely. You meet some woman and just like that" (clicking my fingers) "you build yourself a Sardinian palace which to me seems the best thing you've ever done."

"The built environment, Chuck. The human home." He scratched his head: "Where did I read that?"

"You must be spending money like water but you seem to have more money than ever."

"That's the way money works."

"Not for me it's not."

"Yeah, but you don't understand money, Chuck, you think it's a finite resource, but it's really not. Everywhere you look there's a fucking pile of money just waiting to be picked up, you just have to decide if it's yours. Money doesn't need to run out. Ever. You have to recycle it, spend it, and make it come back to you"

"Fascinating, Jimmy. Bloody fascinating."

"So you want to meet my wife. She's pretty spectacular. But not what you're expecting."

"What am I expecting?"

"American woman. Good body. Yoga, macrobiotic diet, full of Californian sincerity, ultimately not interesting, but a great body, which acts like a counterweight, even though half of it is fucking genetically modified. It's always much easier to be interested in an attractive person, don't you think? You end up playing this game with yourself, laughing at yourself, telling yourself what a simple guy you are because you're prepared to put up with this dead-head who's kind of dumb but nicely predictable. And there's something very articulate about beauty."

"You married a dumb woman because she's beautiful?"

"No, no. I told you, you'll never guess what she's like. You won't know until you meet her."

"Okay. When am I going to meet her?"

"Listen Chuck, have another drink, something stronger than green tea, okay? Something like a caipirinha. Ask the girl downstairs to mix one up for you. Then sit in the whirlpool for a while. There's one on the terrace right outside your bedroom, sit and watch the swifts until you're slightly bored. Boredom is good, remember that! It sets you up for a good evening. Then put on some clean clothes and come down to the dining room. We'll be waiting for you."

"What's her name?"

"It's Archie."

"Where's she from? That's a man's name."

"She's British. Well, Indian-British. Punjabi parents. Now go and clean yourself up. You're a typical Brit. You arrive off a plane, travel for another two hours in a taxi, arrive, crash, get up in the morning, slum around in a dressing gown, and by lunchtime you still haven't had a shower. Go and have a shower. Please."

"How do you know if I showered?"

"I know everything that happens in this house."

I do what he says. I sit in the plunge pool, I watch the swifts and have a drink and start getting bored. The room is stark, not even a television in there. Just a bed, a lamp recessed into the wall, a cupboard recessed into another. One insanely uncomfortable chair made of moulded birch. The doors leading onto the terrace are partially shaded by overhanging eaves, again with carved dragons. The terrace is sharp-edged, and the plunge pool reaches to the edge so that when you're in the water you feel you might tumble off. Peering down, you see another angular terrace just below, also with a pool, this one with dark green plants all round it, lending more shade.

Sardinia is a very hot place. When the sun gets too oppressive I climb out, go inside and top off my glass with whisky from the suitcase; cheap stuff, too aromatic for this heat.

Bloody swifts make a racket, but at least they keep themselves busy.

This is good, better than London.

For a moment I forget myself, and it's a blessing.

II

Although there was no one else in the room I felt we were being watched, almost as if the table were on a stage.

Archie was quite impeccably presented. On her left, Jimmy was vigorously attacking his plate, with grinding jaws. For my part I concentrated on his wife, who unnerved me.

"So you're Archie?"

"I'm not the cleaner."

"Ha-ha! I'm Chuck, good friend of Jimmy's."

"I hope so. Otherwise what are you doing here?"

"Most people come to stay because they're looking for something to bitch about," Jimmy threw in. "Klaus is not like that."

"So I see." There was a pause while she transferred her attention to me. "Are you German?"

She was too damned charming, too much sex appeal. I swallowed my nerves and tried to sound casual. "No. I just had cruel parents with a strange taste in names. Call me Chuck, everyone else does."

Archie's eyes were black and inscrutable, yet also filled with consolation. It made me want to dredge up some long-gone hurt, and tell her all about it. She would have consoled me.

She was wearing a long red dress covered in tiny pieces of mirror-glass; it was cut low across her magnificent orbs, with a hint of glistening black brassiere offering a whiff of the wild country.

I was not, I hasten to add, lusting over my friend's wife. I was aware of her qualities, which is entirely different. Whenever I felt myself quickly tearing my eyes away from what she revealed, I felt her consolation washing over me, carried by a wistful, knowing smile. She was aware of the fact that men are hopelessly, mechanically drawn to a well-made woman, even if that woman is a merciless harpy.

Archie, incidentally, seemed perfectly pleasant. Not a harpy at all.

"So what do you think of my wife?" Jimmy blurted out, eager to hang his clothes-line through the middle of our conversation.

By now we were sitting down, and the maid had just plonked down big white plates with carpaccio of tuna and exquisite arragosto tails.

I smiled and said, with my mouth full: "I never use the third-person when the third person's sitting there, but I think she passes with flying colors."

"Why are English guys always feeding you bull?" Jimmy said, with an uxorious glance at his wife.

"The English are so good at platitude. They spend their lives in it. They get embarrassed if you stray off it," she said.

"Fuck! The platitude of Englishness." Jimmy shook his head. "Makes me glad I'm American."

I cut in. "Look, the English are very passionate people. It's just we're passionate about saying as little as possible. We're passionate about being reserved."

"English men make the best lovers," said Archie. "They're so repressed that they end up being dynamite in bed. They go off like sodding warheads."

"Anyway, you're English," I said. "Don't let Jimmy make you the foreigner."

"When you marry an American who has no country, you learn to deconstruct yourself. It's even easier when you're a second-generation immigrant."

"And you've done it, have you? Deconstructed yourself?"

"Of course. I get to swan around in nice dresses while staff serve me delicious food. Next week we'll be in our flat in Paris. Jimmy will be off working somewhere, maybe his shopping mall in China. Do you know where I grew up, Chuck? In Southall. You know where that is?"

"Of course. Best curries in London."

"Yes. The best curries. That's about it, unless you want a cheap sari."

We ate. The windows were open, and swarms of swifts kept screaming as they darted over the tiled rooftops. I lit a cigarette without asking—guest's privilege—and then sat quietly watching a sculpture in the middle of the table, a circular figure with a hole cut diagonally through the bronze, about forty centimeters high: probably a Henry Moore.

Jimmy put down his fork, drained his glass of wine and looked at his wife. "We haven't told him the most interesting thing about our marriage. Have we?"

They looked at me. I stubbed out my cigarette.

"My wife's a nice-looking woman, right Chuck? Most guys would think we have a great sex life, lots of action every night, no wonder we're always making an excuse to get an early night. Right?"

"But we don't." Archie said. "We don't have a sex life."

"Do you want to rephrase that, honey?" said Jimmy.

"We don't have a normal physical relationship, and by that I mean..."

"We've developed a concept of non-sexual coitus."

I looked from one to the other. "So is this why you invited

me down? To help you sort out your sexual issues?"

"Told you he's great, Archie, you can always rely on him to say something fucking great like that! No, you stupid son-of-a-bitch!"

We smirked at each other, although I was feeling a bit puzzled, then compelled to fish for information. "Maybe you just need a long holiday together, so you can—"

"You don't understand," said Archie. "We have the best sex I've ever had. It's just we don't touch each other. At all."

"It's kind of a mental thing," said Jimmy.

"Sex is too predictable," said Archie. "Totally externalized, not holistic at all."

I turned to Jimmy, and for an instant, I saw the sadness in him, revolving slowly like a dying star throwing out its wavering beams. Aha!

After the late lunch, I made an excuse and went to lie in my plunge pool, vacantly yet with thoughts circulating in my mind, much like the vultures I saw over the yellow mountain at the top of the valley.

III

Call me a simpleton, but if I had a wife like Archie with lovely dark eyes and beautiful curved eyebrows, and a sensual mouth like a jewelled half-moon, bright pearly teeth and long slim arms, her whole body light brown and velvety, fronted by swelling breasts, all borne up by legs of good length but not of the spaghetti variety (personally I have never liked women with limbs like pasta), I would certainly look forward to lying in bed with a book, looking up as she undressed, peeling off her garments one by one and then tiredly climbed into the bed, revealing her soft waist, curving hips and dark bifurcated triangle. I would wrap my arms round her, and we'd both start looking for release in each other's bodies. I would watch her eyes swooning as she gradually lost touch with the night, the particularity of us lying there, the damp soft air, the frogs croaking outside from pools and the mosquitoes wailing like miniature pipes.

It would be just like that. If I had a wife, I mean. I never had a wife of any description. Loneliness holds fewer perils than anything thrown up by togetherness, as exemplified by Jimmy and this gin-trap into which he had so willingly inserted his foot. Mental sex. What sort of nonsense was that? He just had to be suffering. Sure enough, he'd met the woman of his dreams, but this fabled meeting with the love object was not the end but rather the beginning of the quest. Archie had led him into a terrible adventure. Now, although he was bound to her, she was denying him her body, whilst at the same time consoling him and softening the loneliness of existence with her charms. He, brave fool, was making the best of it.

Why were women so corrosive, so dangerous to a man's happiness?

All I could do was to lie there and, in Jimmy's words, listen to the swifts until they started to revolt me.

IV

I was aware of an imminent boredom.

This boredom grew all day without cease. The streets were empty but for old women in their black glad-rags, working at lace-making in the doorways or leaning over bowls of still-steaming white ricotta cheese. No activity, no youth, no vigor, just the regularity of tolling bells, furtive priests and moss sprouting between the paving stones.

The plunge pool became my refuge, my blessing. I lay prostrate in it, a long-suffering look on my face. Heaven does not always conform to our expectations. It does not, for instance, necessarily take the form of a Le Corbusier vision of stark lines, cool vistas, and high-density concrete, nor does it have a New Tibetan influence of over-hanging hardwood eaves and carved beams. In the end, modern architecture is an attempt to overlook the basic human reality. Whether we like it or not we do not dwell in the halls of Olympus.

As I lay there looking up at the pair of elongated, carved serpents above my head, I heard a sound from the terrace below. Because of the angle of the eaves, the sound bounced with perfect clarity. It was a woman's voice, probably Archie's. I listened intently.

"Thank you, angel." That was all she said for a while, but there was emotion in her voice, a nuance that I immediately recognized as sensualized gratitude. "Yes, good, you are finding it. There! Oh God!"

Finally I couldn't contain myself any more. I paddled to the edge of the plunge pool and peered down at the oasis on the terrace below.

What did I see? Not Archie on a beach towel, semi-naked and writhing under Jimmy, vulpine, bursting with virility.

No.

In fact, what I saw was Archie wearing a chaste white toga fastened at her shoulder with a golden clasp, her hair fixed on top of her head, revealing the curvature of her spine and a gracefully arched neck. Jimmy, meanwhile, was in a thick-towelled dressing gown, a rather unfetching little number, dark blue with a sort of striated pattern down the sides.

They were facing each other across a small teak table.

Placed in the middle was the Henry Moore sculpture I had seen at lunch. Jimmy was stroking it with his hand. As he did so, Archie rolled her head and closed her eyes. Jimmy then gently pushed his hand into the hollow, stroking the edges with his fingers. All the time he watched her with an intensity like a boy spying on a woman as she takes off her bra. Archie reacted with a sharp intake of breath. Her nostrils flared, her lips opened in a grimace of pain, almost.

I had seen enough. Quickly I withdrew and lay in a state

of incomprehension, breathing a little too hard. There was a measure of panic, even.

There is a moment when you lose emotional tranquillity. Even if what you had before was acrid and full of bitterness, even if you had nothing much to celebrate, still you miss it: that stasis when you had nothing and expected nothing.

Now I had the image of Archie, the curvature of her spine, her yearning mouth.

The boredom had gone and I missed it.

V

A few hours later I sauntered down an air-conditioned corridor towards the games room, where as usual I found Jimmy lining up a shot at the snooker table. He assumed an air of light-hearted sarcasm towards me, hardly even looking at me. "Chuck, you look wet. So you actually made it into the shower today? Did you find the soap as well?" His long red failed spectacularly, leaving the pot on and spreading the blue and pink disastrously. "Let me ask you something. You think my whole life is one big picnic, right? Just because I have money, a lovely home and an amazing wife? What you don't get about me is that I've suffered. I'm a sufferer. I'm not just rich by accident, I'm rich because I fought for it. I planted this damned money-tree and watched it grow. For years."

"I don't doubt it for a minute, Jimmy. And it doesn't surprise me that you've been depressed. I suppose somewhere down the line you must have realized all the things you fought so hard for were meaningless."

I could have bitten off my tongue. I sounded like a bitter, middle-aged man. It occurred to me that might just be what I was.

Jimmy shook his head. "You sad fuck, Chuck." He smiled bitterly, and repeated himself. "You sad fuck, Chuck. It even rhymes." He tried another shot and failed again. This time he scowled and put down the cue on the felt baize. "You resent me because I've gone for something. I even had to fight for my terrific wife. She didn't just fucking materialize, okay! You think she wanted me when we first met? I'm sixteen years older than her. I'm a workaholic and I'm not good at saying fun things at breakfast. Archie means everything to me. She's the most valuable thing I've got."

"She's not a thing. And you don't own her."

"Don't I know it," said Jimmy, crossing the room and slumping into an aquamarine leather armchair. His telephone made a bleeping sound, and he checked a message before looking up with a distracted expression. "I often wake up before dawn, then lie there thinking about the things missing in my life. Take a guy like you, Chuck, you're broke and haven't got a hell of a lot going on, but I'd rather be in your shoes than mine. You know why? Because you seem basically content to be a sad bastard. I'd shoot myself if I had to wake up in the morning and be you."

I poured myself a drink and tried to mask my irritation with the self-satisfied prick. All I could do was hit him back with all the sarcasm I had.

"I don't know if you have a terrific wife, Jimmy, I haven't seen enough of her. All I know is she has a fondness for modern sculpture."

"Oh I think you've seen enough. She's the sort of woman you'd kill for."

There was a long silence. I decided to play it straight. "So that's what you do? You touch a sculpture, and she imagines you're touching her body?"

"The sculpture is just an aid. She doesn't imagine it. She actually feels it. With intensity."

"I didn't mean to spy on you."

"Don't fret, man. We knew you were there all along."

"You did?"

"Sure. We're kind of high on this thing, we've invented a

new way of having sex. We want to tell the world, it could be our greatest achievement."

"What would Billy Graham make of you, I wonder?"

"He'd hate us. We'd put him out of a job."

"He'd find a way of damning you. Adultery is in the mind, that's what he'd say."

"And he'd be right."

"Jimmy, do you never just feel like getting between your wife's legs and fucking her normally?"

"No way. Not at all," he said, his eyes full of waspish sincerity. "More importantly, Archie wouldn't like it. She doesn't like penetration."

"That's what she tells you?"

"We fucked on our wedding night and after that maybe a half-dozen times. Sometimes I wonder if she finds my cock uncomfortable? I pack a bit of a punch, you know."

He moved up to the window, where he stood looking out into the sunlit glare, listening to the thudding tennis balls from a court at the back of the house. Archie, in white ankle-socks and a short white skirt, was fiercely hitting ground-strokes to an opponent hidden behind a juniper hedge. As she slid across the clay court, throwing up palls of ochre dust, I lost myself in her physical presence—her swinging hair, eager grunts, and bronzed smooth legs, lithe as Chris Evert's at her early-career best—and reminded myself I hadn't slept with a woman for eighteen months.

I grew aware of Jimmy blinking self-consciously at me. In a forlorn voice, he said, "Chuck, are you attracted to my wife?"

Attraction to me conjures up a horseshoe magnet covered in iron filings. Not a pair of lovers joined at the hip. "Christ, Jimmy, what's the matter with you? Of course I'm not!"

"But you find her attractive?"

"Okay, yes, she's attractive, I can't lie about that, but you must have known that when you married her. Or did you think no one would ever look at her again because she was married?"

"No, but she's very animal, and it hurts when—"

"Has it ever occurred to you that what you need is to have a child?"

He stared at me, startled, disturbed. "I'm not sure that would be such a good idea. We're very busy. It's a lot of responsibility." He stopped and fidgeted. "Is that what you'd do if you were married to my wife? Have a child with her?"

"Jimmy! What's happened to you? Yes, I would have a child with her. You've got money, just get yourself a Philippino nanny, enjoy your marriage! Because yes, you have a lovely wife and if you're not careful you're going to lose her. I mean what woman would be satisfied with this?"

This time it was Jimmy's turn to be incredulous. He threw out his arms and laughed. "Come on, what's wrong with this? We have everything."

"Your wife's not happy, okay? She's a beautiful woman full of life and energy. And very bright too. She's got a sexual neurosis of some kind, and you should get some therapeutic help. And then have a child."

"That's what you think? Interesting." He nodded. "Because we have this problem. I mean I have a problem."

"Yes?"

"I think she's looking for an affair."

"And that surprises you?" I waited a good minute, then blurted out: "Jimmy, I have to say this is totally insane. I mean, what the hell are you getting involved with, this whole mental sex thing? Isn't it just some stupid idea you cooked up because things weren't working between you?"

"Sigmund Freud said successful creative people sublimate their physical urges."

"Yes, but Freud was insane."

"So is everyone, Chuck. So is everyone."

He stood there for a moment, clutching his head as if he were afraid it was going to fly away. I regretted my hard words to him.

"It'll be okay, Jimmy. Don't worry."

"Chuck, it's good to have you here. Sincerely."

He blinked his watery eyes at me, and I understood this was the moment when I had to put my hand on his shoulder and give it a little shake while making a sort of intense grimace of affection.

He hugged me and apologized for giving me a hard time, assuring me that he didn't mean it like that. He was just stressed, there was too much to do at the office and it looked like he had to go to China tomorrow.

"China!"

"Yeah, you've heard of China, right? Biggest bullshit factory in the world. You get paid in cash but you've got to pull it out of people's asses."

"So what'll I do then?" I said. "I can't just stay here with Archie, I wouldn't feel comfortable."

"Why not?" he said without enthusiasm. "Stay, relax, enjoy the servants and the house and the pools and terraces. I'll go and fucking work like I always do. I mean someone's got to pay for all this shit. Yeah. Just one thing, Chuck. One thing, okay, and I'm not asking a lot here. If she comes to you and wants you to go to bed with her just tell her no. Tell her you're my friend and she's got to respect that."

His anxious eyes pored over me, and I wished I'd stayed in London where nothing ever happened.

VI

After he'd gone, I stayed there in the window for a while, magnetized by the shining white figure in the garden. Then I opened the door to the wooden decking outside and walked down the teak steps to the path. Like a wraith drawn by a power greater than itself, I felt myself moving towards the tennis court, where Archie grew aware of me.

"Hello there, Chuck!" she called out. "You play tennis?"

I stopped by the wire netting. "No. I don't like games."

"Oh, you should get into them." She smashed a forehand down the line. "Me and Jimmy are crazy about games."

"I noticed."

Waving to her opponent, a short, hairy-legged Sard who turned out to be the gardener, she came up to me, wiping the sweat from her face. "Jimmy's going away."

"He told me."

"And so I was thinking if you can keep your wits about it, we could have an affair."

I was flummoxed, absolutely flummoxed. It was like she'd suggested we should watch some television, or go for a walk together. "An affair? And what would Jimmy have to say about that?"

"Jimmy's got to grow up!" said Archie. "Anyway, it's up to you. I've made you an offer, and you can either decline or accept. Just think of it as a great chance to get some exercise." She smiled.

I shook my head like a frowning schoolmaster. "You know I came out here to relax. I came thinking that Jimmy had settled down with a woman he loved."

"He does love me. I'm not sure I love him so very much but at least I'm not leaving him. Not yet anyway."

"You two are a fucking recipe for divorce."

"If you don't want to do it, that's fair enough. You seem a sensible bloke, Chuck, and I like that." She grabbed the wire-netting fence with both hands. "I expect you're probably the kind of man who doesn't like a straight offer, but I don't have very much time. So just tell me if you want me or not."

I looked at her and I did want her, although it was all fairly abstract. "Yes. Not very fair to Jimmy, though, is it?"

"Oh it's very fair. I'll tell you more about it later. Maybe."

She waited for my answer, and finally I nodded. "Okay, if that's what you want."

"Good. You're sure?"

"I'm not sure. I can't be sure until this whole thing's played itself out, but I'm saying okay for now."

Her eyes were still consoling. Now those eyes seemed to say: relax, take me, do what you want.

"Don't make such a big thing of it. It's really not. You don't have to marry me or anything."

"Maybe for you it's something very normal. Maybe you do this stuff all the time. You know when I first met you I thought you seemed a straightforward woman with a good mind. I was a bit confused, though—do you mind my saying that?—about you and Jimmy. What you were doing with him."

"You have a pretty low opinion of your friend, don't you?"

"I suppose so."

"And of me as well?" She loomed over me when she said that, the sun catching the shine of her black hair.

"I don't have a low opinion of you at all."

"Thanks." She stuck her finger through the netting and wiggled it at me. "So you want to go ahead with this thing?"

"I told you yes. Just stop talking about it like some sort of project. But I'm not getting involved in this whole mental sex thing. I make love normally, so don't bring some damned sculpture to bed, because I'll walk out. This is all a bit of a mind-fuck, if you don't mind me saying so."

"Chuck, get out of the taboo, get inside the emotion. Okay?"

Christ, this woman had spent too long in America! I stared at her, then tried to control my disquiet. "When do you want to start?"

"Tomorrow. We'll have a light supper at about six, then we'll rest for a half hour and meet here on the terrace afterwards. One other thing, Chuck. Try to remember that I will be working through a number of different sexual attitudes."

"How do you mean, attitudes?"

"You'll see. I won't be myself. Not quite."

"Like a role-play thing? Will you come in wearing black leather and thigh-length boots?"

"Would you like me to?"

"No. Not at all. Just wear the red dress you wore last night."

VII

The next day, after we'd eaten and Jimmy had left and said his despondent farewells, I almost sighed with delight when I saw her. She'd conspired to look exactly as she did the first night I saw her. Women understand these things. Her hair was up, revealing that soft arching neck with the soft earlobes pierced by gold rings. Even the tiny piercings excited me, the way they broke through the soft rotunda of flesh. Her lips were slightly tensed—sexual excitement or just plain nervousness?

"So. Here you are. In your entirety," I said.

"Not quite," she said. "Remember, flesh is a veil. Come over here, sit down. Take a closer look at me."

I sat down beside her. No longer forbidden fruit, she now seemed a woman like any other. Certainly beautiful, but otherwise perfectly ordinary. When she leaned back and smiled invitingly at me, I felt coerced by the situation. She noticed immediately.

"You preferred me when I was not available?" she said.

"Oh, infinitely."

We sat in silence. Then she shook her head. "You see. Words are such a turn-off."

After that we kissed for a while. To be frank, I found her slimy tongue rather repellent, the way it insistently pumped in and out of my mouth. She maintained this for about ten minutes, then put her hand on my crotch.

"Archie. This is not working for me," I said.

She gave me a murderous look, slid down on the floor, unzipped me and parted my legs, then fellated me until it became necessary for me to issue a little cautionary note, which she ignored, keeping her eyes firmly drilled into mine throughout the whole ghastly experience.

She rolled onto the sofa, sighed with relief and rested her head in my lap. "That was the first part," she said. "I can file that away now. For later use."

I was still hyperventilating. "Mental sex?"

"Correct." She looked at me. "I may never need to suck cock again for as long as I live."

I smiled, finding myself a little more at ease with her, and the situation. "What would Jimmy have to say about that?"

"Oh let's not talk about him."

After a few minutes she started peeling off her clothes. She was every bit as exquisite as I had thought. Her dun skin was velvety, and down below, her dark hair had been carefully shaved to reveal a dusky, sensitized ridge.

Before long she was straddling me, revolving her powerful haunches and grinding herself against me. Surprisingly, I revived instantly. I felt her pubic bone, her sharpness against my crotch, as we contracted and pulsed together.

I was a man of forty-four, but never in my whole life had I had such a powerful erotic experience. Yet however hard I worked, Archie never seemed quite satisfied. She would roll onto her back, parting her legs as if to cool the super-heated gates to her musk-scented kingdom.

At one point when I was brazen enough to suggest we might take a coffee-break, maybe with a few biscuits or a leg of lamb or something, she grinned at me and said, "Fine, but first I could go for another go."

I felt myself glaring at her, in disbelief. "Don't you ever get tired?"

"What do you want me to do? I like fucking. I like fucking with you. Amazing, isn't it? Poor old Scrooge, he can't accept the good things life offers him." Her gorgeous amber-hued eyes glowed at me. I felt I had never seen anything quite so beautiful in all my life. I inclined my head and pressed my lips reverentially to her hand.

These antics continued for several days, all heady and new. I didn't need any encouragement, almost felt I was receiving an education. I found myself confronting a sort of prurience in myself, confirming something I had always known: I am no sexual explorer. For instance, it gave me no great pleasure to have to penetrate her from behind, whilst she straddled the floor like a dog and exposed her odoriferous rump. Call me a prude, but I have no great regard for such practices.

In the evenings, after these sexual marathons, we ate plenty of beef and seafood and salad, then slept like Trojans.

After a week I was exhausted. By the seventh day, the mere sight of her made me feel like a galleon slave at the approach of the Empress.

VIII

Finally, we had the post-mortem.

"I think your feelings for me have abated somewhat," she said.

"I'm tired, I suppose."

"It's so much more than that, Chuck. Isn't it?"

"It's exhaustion."

"No. It's *matter*."

I looked at her, interested in spite of myself. "What do you mean by that?"

"The inherent imperfection of matter." She flashed a sudden smile. "The old dualist problem. The body is the abode of the incarcerated soul, doomed to wait for its release. Every sexual act, even within the bonds of marriage, is a spiritual transgression."

"Are you serious?"

"The way I see sex is, it's a degrading act between two people looking for misplaced ecstasy. In the end, the unfortunate by-product of sex is another imprisoned soul subject to the very same pull of Lucifer; and so the world of matter prolongs itself, like an alcoholic who can't stop drinking."

"Does sex really have to be so very degrading? I mean, are you sure you're not exaggerating all this. Is it really so bad, so awful?"

Archie pursed her lips. "Look. For a week we fucked each other's brains out. Now what? What is there between us?"

"Physical intimacy?"

"No. When you met me you thought me wonderful. You said so to Jimmy. You admired me. Now I'm no longer any use to you. You don't even like me particularly."

"I do like you perfectly well, Archie. But it's all been a bit impersonal, hasn't it?"

"Chuck, I don't think you've ever felt for any woman what you feel for me. You have to be much more honest emotionally if you want to avoid the fate of millions of your fellow Englishmen. You know, all those sad blokes down the pub drinking bitter and pretending they care about the cricket scores."

That was the last meaningful conversation we had for a long time. The only tangible result of the week was that my stomach seemed flatter and I had to take my belt in a notch.

Soon I was packed and gone. London received me in its cool, disinterested embrace. I was back on Pudding Island, eating muffins and drinking Darjeeling with acquaintances all apparently eager to discuss David Hare's latest play. There were chestnuts roasting outside the British Museum and, on every street corner, free newspapers stuffed with information about those fascinating princes Harry and Will, the rigors of Afghanistan and Robbie Williams's Ferrari collection.

Oh dear, oh fuck! What a load of second-hand nonsense.

I always wanted the world to be a little wilder than this.

IX

The trouble with sexual experiments, however consensual, is that they tend to destroy friendships.

I didn't see Jimmy and Archie for about a year and a half after the events I have related. Then I bumped into Jimmy in Berlin, at an art fair. By then Jimmy and Archie had divorced, and Archie had spent several months living in Sai Baba's ashram in India, before coming back to Europe, weighed down by dubious spiritual baggage.

Jimmy's attitude to me was vaguely hostile, but not as much as I'd expected. I ate a hell of a lot of humble pie, while he stood there smiling at me then cut me off in the middle of my apologetic ramblings.

"I knew what she was planning all along, Chuck. She'd already told me she liked you."

"She had?"

"Yeah. I knew you wouldn't be able to resist her. She said you were perfect because you wouldn't get too involved. Or pester her afterwards. The perfect English gentleman. She had you figured, Chuck."

"So you really knew?"

"Kind of." He slapped me on the shoulder. "Who cares? It's all old hat now."

Nothing had changed, in fact. There was still me in my moleskin trousers and scuffed brogues, and there was Jimmy, the great glittering pretend-shark, with a bloodless wound somewhere about his person.

"Were you very disappointed when it all messed up?"

He looked at me, an astonished smile on his face. "Me? Of course not! I was fucking relieved, man! I was sick of all the games, the whole mental sex thing. Women are players. They analyze the game stats. Men just want to win and get it over with. I'm no different from all the rest."

"How is Archie?"

"Oh. Fucking crazy, of course! The divorce has been a hell of a ride."

"Must have cost you a bit?"

"It did. I had to give her the house in Sardinia. She's living there now. I'm still picking up the tab. She's pretty well going nuts, I reckon."

"Poor Archie," I said, surprising myself. "So do you miss your life there in Sardinia?"

"To be honest I couldn't stand the place. All that stinky old cheese, peasants on mopeds. Fucking creepy, wasn't it?" I sensed his wound again, carefully hidden under his crumpled linen Armani suit. "What about you? Any last thoughts about Archie?"

His question set me off. At once I was back in that bed by the window, the low sunlight pouring in: Archie, her honey-colored skin, the little soft hairs round her belly-button. I felt myself quickening at the very thought of her.

"I'd like to see Archie some time. I grew to like Archie very much."

He smirked, distinctly ill-at-ease. "She told me you didn't like her very much at all, actually."

"She did?"

"You were relieved to get the hell out of there. That's what she said."

"Yeah, but given the situation. I was racked with guilt, Jimmy."

He came in closer, his pale eyebrows beetling. He said, "So you felt you did wrong, did you?"

"Of course I did. But she threw herself at me. I..."

"Stop!" He nodded at a good-looking blonde making her way towards us, a ferocious grin on her fake-tan face. "There's my new wife right there. You want to meet her?"

"No offense, Jimmy, but I've got to go, if you know what I mean."

"Don't worry, Chuck. This one likes fucking. Physically."

Before I could slip away, she'd pulled up in front of us. She was Californian, with a good body, a frightening level of earnestness and an interest in yoga and macrobiotics. All this came out in the first two minutes.

"I feel we've met somewhere before," I said.

"No, no, no!" she cried, grasping my arm fiercely as if to show me what a tactile person she was. "You're getting me confused with someone else out there. And I'm very typically Californian. I mean this is actually real blonde hair!"

"Oh yeah, that's real blonde hair all right!" Jimmy confirmed, with a grin.

"But apart from that there's not so much that stands out about me."

"Oh I don't know about that," said Jimmy, giving her rump a little playful slap. She shrieked with delight, baring her teeth in a way that would have provoked an attack among chimpanzees. Then said to me, without irony: "He's so cute! I just love Danny de Vito types. Short, overweight professionals." Pecking him on the cheek, she confided further: "You know he's the kind of guy who can't leave the airport without buying you a pair of diamond studs."

Jimmy looked at me. "So, where are you off to in such a hurry? Can't you stay and have dinner with us at least?"

"Yeah!" his wife cried. "Come On! Have Dinner With Us!"

I glanced at Jimmy, and it occurred to me that he looked old, tired, gone to seed, with thrombotic cheeks and watering eyes. "I'm sorry. I've got to get home and pack."

"Oh yeah, where you going?" his wife asked.

Their faces dropped like blinds when I told them. "It's been on my mind for a while. I think it's time I went back to Sardinia."

X

I never expected to go back to the Cathar pavilion, but what one expects is largely worthless, in my experience.

After the plane had touched down, as I crossed the tarmac into the terminal building I was already feeling the island's powerful enchantment. The low-slung hills seemed to brood against the evening sky, and the air was pungent with wild herbs. A flock of mysterious birds arrowed through the fading light.

Standing in line by the passport control, I noticed a series of swallows' nests—encrusted, homely balls under the eaves of the main building. One of the nests had fallen and dashed itself against the ground. It lay in smithereens all round our feet, covered in crawling insects. On the wall I counted a straight line of seven green moths, like a motif taken from a Carey Mortimer fresco. Beneath them lurked a tiny lizard, but indecision marred its progress, and it did not move.

By the time I had picked up my suitcase, rented a car and stopped off for a snack it was approaching midnight. I had not told Archie I was coming. In fact I had specifically not told Archie I was coming, otherwise I could of course have telephoned. When you forewarn people, you give them the chance of acting the hypocrite. Or of saying no.

But it was a bit much arriving unannounced at two in the morning. Wasn't it?

In the end, that was precisely how it turned out.

I left the luggage in the boot and walked through a jumble of tiny, dark lanes under a yellow, oversized moon. Thousands of moths were bombarding the metal covers of the streetlights with a sickeningly insistent sound, like tiny fingers against drums.

The abandoned piazzas, the shuttered houses, all seemed to be under the spell of this infernal sound. I erupted in goose bumps, then forced myself to stand there and watch the moths. They traced concentric circles in the air, like a Paul Nash painting of dogfights over Kent.

I realized what it all reminded me of. Chimes. Buddhist gongs. Archie in a white toga on the terrace—the sexualization of enlightenment?

I stood on a corner, gazing up and muttering to myself until I noticed a man in a singlet smoking out of a window. He did not acknowledge me, but must have found me strange. I walked on, embarrassed.

Towards the top of the town I saw the white dome of Jimmy's house, now Archie's. It glowed under the moon. Her window was lit, or at least there was a lit window and I assumed it must be hers. This cheered me greatly, as I had not wanted to make my entrance as a sort of Walter de la Mare traveller beating on the door of an empty, preternatural house.

There was a bell but it seemed rude to use it at that late hour. Instead I picked up some pebbles and began to throw them at the window. After a couple of direct hits, a figure appeared on the edge of one of the terraces. Archie, with her hair unkempt, like Cassandra on the battlements.

"I told you, clear off! Scram! Got it?"

"Archie. It's me! Chuck!"

"Chuck! What are you doing here?"

"I'm not quite sure at the moment. Can I come in?"

"Yes, of course. Why didn't you call?"

"I didn't have time," I said somewhat illogically. "Can I come in please? I'm shattered."

It took five minutes for her to come down. "Sorry," she said. "Bloody stairs." As she walked into the lit-up hall I realized something had changed about her. She looked tired and sad, in a slightly grotty dressing gown. Gone was the femme fatale, but then what woman can keep it up round the clock?

"How are you, Archie?"

"What are you doing here?"

"I just wanted to see how you were."

"Is that all? I hope Jimmy didn't send you."

"Where can I sleep?"

"Not with me."

"Of course not."

"What do you mean, of course not? We used to sleep together, didn't we?"

"Yes, but only for a week. And that was a year ago."

A weary expression crossed her face. "I'm actually quite glad you're here. Do you know that?"

"Who did you think I was?"

"Oh some Australian berk who keeps pestering me."

I didn't ask her anything else for the time being. She led me into one of the guest rooms, then, after a bit of idle conversation, said good night.

The bed was gritty with breadcrumbs or sand or both, and the sheets had been drenched in sweat on a few occasions. They smelled of feet, but I was too tired to care. It felt absolutely right that I should be there. I lay there for a while, wiggling my toes under those unclean sheets with a real sense of achievement. As yet I didn't know why.

All I could say with certainty was that I was here to do good.

XI

I was woken up at a quarter past seven by Archie standing at the foot of the bed.

"Do you want coffee?" she said.

My eyelids opened like lead coffin-lids. "Coffee?" Her question seemed absurd, as if she'd offered me some roast chicken.

"I suppose you'll be wanting toast and jam, being a bit of an English chap. Oh but of course, how could I forget? You like a cooked breakfast. You're a bacon man, aren't you? With poached eggs and devilled kidneys?"

"Archie! What are you doing?"

She blinked. "Oh I don't know. I'm bored. I couldn't sleep." She sat down on the bed with a sigh. "Everything is so difficult now."

I looked round, taking in the cobwebs and dust everywhere. An abandoned, half-filled cup of tea in a corner had gone rank, covered in a film of green mold. This tendency was replicated on the terrace, which had grown a covering of moss. The once-pristine plunge-pool now looked more like a garden pond suitable for goldfish.

"I suppose the cleaners have gone?"

"Yes. Jimmy won't pay the alimony. He's bitter about things. His new wife is an heiress. They're loaded."

"He did give you the house, though."

"Only because he didn't want it. He hates this place. Anyway, what's a house? It's just a pile of stone, with a roof on top. Somewhere you can put your things. A house isn't food or money. Speaking of which, do you mind doing some shopping? I'm flat broke."

"Yes, in a minute." I refocused on the problem. "It's a big house, though. You could sell it."

"This pile of shit? It leaks, and the municipality is challenging the planning permission. They say it was obtained illegally. I suppose Jimmy greased someone's palm. That's what he always does. No one would ever buy it. The trouble with you and all English people is that you think too much about houses. You think I'm fine because I've got a house, don't you? Meanwhile I could be hanging myself, but at least I've got a house to leave to my children. Except I don't even have any bloody children thanks to fucking Jimmy. Bastard." At this point her lips began to quiver.

"Well, mental sex was hardly going to prove very useful in that respect, was it? Although by the time we have children most of us are already going mental, it's got to be admitted."

Archie closed her eyes in exasperation. "Oh shut up, Chuck, you talk like a bloody queer sometimes! You'd never get a woman pregnant, would you? You'd never lose control, and you'd never fuck anyone unless you were wearing a triple-glazed fucking condom. You're not passionate, you're derivative. That's why you never got anywhere in the arts! I suppose you're some kind of editor."

"I haven't been as unsuccessful as some!" I threw back. "And I did come here to see you, which counts for something, doesn't it?"

There was a pause, then, with much rolling of eyes, she said, "Oh Chuck! What do you know about children anyway?"

"Not much, thank God," I said.

"So spare me your wisdom. Can I tell you something about Jimmy instead? Can I?"

"If you like."

"Don't get sniffy just because I say what I think. That's why you came, isn't it? To find out the truth?"

"Is it?"

"Oh balls! I'm going to tell you about Jimmy whether you like or not." She dropped her voice, as if what she were saying were shameful. "Jimmy was impotent. Completely. There was something wrong with his you know what. It just hung there. It took a bloody miracle to get it up. No wonder my cheekbones looked slightly hollow back then. My cheek-muscles were bloody buff."

"Let's stay off the subject of sex and try to be constructive," I said.

"Oh stop it you old fag! Why is it better?"

"I'm not a fag, Archie. And by the way, I'm not an editor either. I'm a publisher."

"Who cares, Chuck? Who except you in this world actually cares what job you do? We were talking about sex. We only ever talk about sex. I'm not available for that sort of thing any more. I'm not into it."

"You never were, as far as I can see, apart from some histrionics."

"Fuck you, Chuck. You're a real bitch."

"It's just the way I talk."

"No, it's the way you think and it's the way you feel about people, and it's really sad to see a man in his best years all twisted up like this. It's boarding school, isn't it? Being held down and fucked up the arse at thirteen. Not a good start, right?"

We sat in silence. I was awake now, looking out at the terrace. Funny, now that the place was crumbling I actually preferred it. It had taken on some soul.

"So why didn't he just take Viagra?"

"He did sometimes."

"And?"

"Oh it was bloody awful. Like going to bed with a broomstick."

"His new wife seemed happy enough."

"How do you know? Did you fuck her as well?"

"No, Jimmy said he'd never let me near her."

She paused, rubbed her eyes, and said, "So in the end we gave up sex. I wanted to save the marriage so I came up with mental sex. Jimmy went for it, or played along with it, more likely."

"Shame. I thought it was an interesting concept."

"It would have been interesting if it had worked. I guess Jimmy felt divorce would have been too expensive. Anyway we only saw each other for a few days now and then. He must have been seeing other women." She nodded to herself. "He probably just found me totally repugnant."

"I doubt that, Archie. You're gorgeous."

"I don't need bolstering," she said. "But thanks all the same."

"Then I came along. And I liked you, didn't I?"

"Yes, that's when I saw my chance to stir things up."

"Did it?"

"You've no idea. Jimmy was more or less deranged. Poor guy, it must be hard not to be able to get your cock up. It's the revenge of all women, isn't it? First no orgasms, then childbirth."

I stood up, and started putting on yesterday's clothes. "Think I'll go and buy some breakfast things."

"Nothing's open yet. Come and have stale bread. We can toast it. And I think there's tea. No fresh milk though, only UHT."

"Delicious."

"When you do go out, if you see a scruffy guy with a beard following you, don't speak to him."

"Who is he?"

"Some guy I met in India at the ashram."

"Is he dangerous?"

"No, just mad. And he loves me. Avoid him, please."

She stood up and left the room. I shuffled along behind her, slightly disgruntled and wondering why I had come. Why had I come, why had I come? Was it just the sex we'd had, the intimacy? If so, I had been an utter fool. This woman was so over me she might as well be a cloud drifting above, oblivious to my pathetic longings.

XII

Archie's warning was apt. When I got to the place known locally as the supermarket, which was about the size of a London tobacconist's, there was a man following me, or at least watching me from the deli counter: a bearded, emaciated ginger-nut with dirty long hair and anxious, pale-blue eyes. He looked like a nervous stork in a wig and sandals.

I confronted him politely. "May I help you?"

He stepped back, as if I'd assaulted him. Then said, in a Pythonesque manner, "What? Help me? Do you want to help me?"

"I asked you a question. I said, may I help you?"

"That's just Pom for fuck off. I know that much." His eyes were watering so profusely they looked in danger of dissolving.

"Who are you? Why are you following Archie?"

"Why do you care? And what's it got to do with you?" He was puffing himself up now, hostile and self-righteous.

"I'm her friend and I am here to help her."

"Oh, that sounds like me! She needs help, conniving bitch! You'll see for yourself." His unwashed face loomed close, whispering, "If I run into you again I won't be so understanding, old chap!"

"Is that a threat?"

He smiled, showing a set of yellow fangs. "Oh dear, not so

big now, are you! Want me to get you some nappies?" Then he walked out.

Nervously I bought eggs, prosciutto, pecorino cheese, green tomatoes, olives, espresso coffee, tea, semi-skimmed milk, cheap table wine, a bottle of good Grappa, three loaves of bread, pasta, biscuits, toilet rolls, sponges and a few other items, then, keeping my eyes open for assailants with blunt weapons, headed back to the Bond pod.

Archie was waiting by the front door when I walked in.

"He was there, wasn't he?" she said. "You spoke to him."

"How did you know?"

"He came steaming down the road about ten minutes ago, stood below in the lane shouting obscenities, then threw a stone."

"Something about this house makes people want to throw stones at it."

"He broke a window. I told you not to speak to him! He's mad."

"You said he wasn't dangerous, remember! By the way, he said you were a conniving bitch, and I'd find out soon enough."

Archie closed the door and bolted it. We threaded our way through a bewildering sequence of open-plan rooms as she spoke over her shoulder: "Of course he did. Men always say that sort of thing when you leave them."

"What were you doing with him in the first place?"

"Do shut up, Chuck."

We entered the stainless steel kitchen, which was exactly like a restaurant kitchen except for the show-off fittings, slate worktops, brash and branded appliances and brass grilles sunk into a fuck-off limestone floor. The windows overlooked the boundary of the town, marked out by a high stone wall. On the other side was a hillside garden where old men grew flowers, beans and artichokes. Beyond them a few mountains, then the sea hovering under the sky.

Everything was a bloody mess, of course. Once people get used to having staff they're always inordinately lazy. I put the things in the fridge after I had cleared out some rotten items and given it a wipe-down with one of the new sponges.

Archie seemed oblivious to my bustling activity. She sat on the worktop, frowning. "I've just realized I completely hate him," she said. "I thought he was just an annoyance. My God, I'm starting to think he could be the biggest problem of all. At least Jimmy doesn't come round to throw stones at the house."

"You'd better come back with me to London. Hadn't you?" I said.

"What for?"

"To avoid being killed?"

"Don't be silly," she sniggered. "Bertie's crazy about me. All he'd do is try and rape me in his very own, inept way."

"Oh, rape you, that's all right then. My God, it's a seesaw world with you, isn't it! One bloke can't get it up, the next one wants to rape you." I looked round, exasperated. "Archie, do you ever wash up?"

"What's the point. Things just get dirty again."

"We'll have to call the cleaner later. I'll pay her myself."

"We can't. I owe her two hundred euro. Let's go upstairs."

We headed up the spiral staircase. Over my shoulder I said, "So, this Bertie? What was he doing in India?"

"Finding God."

"And in the end all he found was little old you. Poor little mite."

"He got confused, didn't he?"

She led me into Jimmy's "thinking room"—that was his name for it. If the room wasn't exactly bursting with intellectual energy, it was certainly an inflated expression of money, that commodity so desired in the world but only ever obtained by a small minority who, once they've attained it, immediately start fretting and convincing themselves they're broke.

I stopped in the doorway, impressed in spite of myself.

The room was large but broken up by a pair of sofas, cream-colored and spotlessly clean. Quite exquisite. Joined seamlessly onto the back of them were flimsy screens of woven silk that stretched up in an organic Spiderman design, until they merged with the ceiling, They were studded with bands of various colors and functioned almost as see-through partitions.

There was an electric fireplace set into the wall, its silvery back studded with crystals turned on by flicking a switch on the wall. It had two settings, each marked with a symbol, one for heat and another for light. The light it gave off had a sort of rippling, lunar effect. It drove me insane.

"This is stunning," I said. "Really!"

"The thing about Jimmy was that he found it hard to live with normal furniture," said Archie. "He didn't like furniture."

"Oh he seemed to like it well enough," I said, with slight venom. "I suppose he got an interior designer to do all this?"

"No, he hates them as well. He chose everything himself. In New York."

I sat down heavily in the sofa, flummoxed by this airy pocket of controlled perfection, while at the same time infuriated by the self-regard of the rich, their anally retentive need for opulence and everything just right.

"If you have a mind you don't need all this. Do you?" I said.

"Jimmy has a mind. As you know, Chuck. It's just a mind that's very concerned with things."

There was a silence, while my eyes dwelt on Jimmy's investments. Leaning against the wall by the window were seven large beaten copper panels decorated with concentric circles, some of them breaking right through the copper, others scratched into the surface. Again, totally exquisite, and this time I happened to recognize them. They were by Jacob Verlaine, a voguish New York artist. A pair of them had recently sold for forty thousand dollars at Sotheby's. One of the panels lay on the floor, with a chair carelessly placed on top of it and an empty tea-cup.

"Have you been sitting on that? You shouldn't. They're very valuable."

"Oh who gives a monkey's about his stuff?"

I lifted the chair away and picked up the panel. The chair-leg had made an imprint in the copper. Carefully I leaned it beside the others.

"No one will even notice," said Archie with a yawn.

At the opposite end of the room was a semi-bald, Egyptian cat lying on one of the sofas. I only noticed it when it started making retching sounds.

"Oh dear," said Archie. "She's not well, I think she ate something funny."

I went over and picked it up with distaste—I have to admit I hate cats—and threw it out of the door. "Archie! You have to wake up. You must start sorting the situation out! You can't just vandalize the place and live here like a down-and-out!"

"Oh shut up!"

"You shut up! Listen to me! If you don't, you're finished."

"I am finished. I wanted to be with Jimmy, I wanted to have a child with him," she wailed.

"Why the hell did you marry an impotent man if you wanted a child?"

"He wasn't impotent at the beginning. He just became impotent. And the more impotent he became, the more determined he was to marry me. And then I spent years making love to a fucking snail!"

"Archie! I'm beginning to think you made him impotent."

"Oh for God's sake, you're really offending me now."

By this point I was standing over her, looking down at her upturned face. How sad to think there had been a time when she drove me to distraction. I grabbed her wrists. "Do you enjoy driving men berserk?"

"You prick, you're no different from the rest of them! Go on then, fuck me! I don't even care."

I pushed her back into the sofa, pinned her down and forced my knee between her legs. Then I came to my senses, let go of her and sat down next to her. "Sorry, I don't know what happened."

She jumped up and tried to run out of the room, but I grabbed her again and we grappled on the floor. Finally we got tired and just lay there.

"I had an abortion," she finally said blearily. "A month ago."

"Oh. Jimmy's?"

"No. Bertie's."

"I thought you wanted a child."

"Not his."

"Does he know?"

"Who?"

"Bertie."

"No, not yet."

"Are you going to tell him?"

"I suppose he'll work it out for himself."

"Couldn't you write him a letter?"

"I don't want to encourage him." She looked at me. "You won't do that again, will you Chuck? I felt safe with you. Now I'm not sure."

"I'm sorry, I don't know where that came from." There was a long pause before I said, quite decisively, "Archie. You're going to have to come with me to London. We'll bring all the art and valuables. We'll have a removals company bring it to London and put it into storage. And we'll have to find you a lawyer."

"I can't possibly pay for all that."

"I'll pay somehow. You can pay me back later."

She broke into sobs, and I left her to it. Practical matters seemed a useful diversion from all this. "By the way, Archie, what happened to that little Rodin sculpture, the one you were using as a—"

"Yes, I know the one you mean. It's not a Rodin, by the way."

"Where is it?"

"I don't know. I threw it at him."

"You did what?"

"I threw it at Jimmy. I missed and it landed in the plunge pool, I think. On the terrace outside our bedroom. Unless it bounced into the street."

We went up another flight of stairs, into the matrimonial bedroom and onto the terrace. A strong, cooling mistral was blowing, blasting us as soon as I opened the sliding glass doors. A similar fate had befallen this plunge pool as the one upstairs. The surface was covered in green algae, and small insects darted about. My arm was submerged up to my armpit as I rummaged about. Finally I pulled it out—a hoary marine treasure out of the depths of time.

When I turned triumphantly to show it to Archie, her face was rather remote and conflicting, and her eyes glimmered darkly as she looked at this dripping object in my hand. I stared at her fixed, unmoving profile. Then realized what should have been plainly obvious right from the very start.

I was in love with Archie. Overpoweringly in love! Just to have her standing close to me was burning up my nerves.

All the same I was aware that my role from here on was platonic. I had to watch her from a distance, sexless and avuncular. Castrated, in fact!

Ah, what dusty answers our souls receive!

We took the sculpture down to the kitchen and cleaned it up with washing-up liquid and a sponge. Later I looked it up in an arts encyclopaedia, and found it was worth over twenty thousand dollars. Damned, sterile money! It meant nothing!

Filled with morose thoughts, this eunuch went back to his room, drank some grappa and slept.

XIII

The days that followed were very busy:

I spoke to a *notario* about the planning dispute with the municipality, and was assured that the matter was largely political and could be resolved by means of delicate negotiations and a modest sum of money. This was duly deposited in the appropriate pocket. An inventory of the contents of the house was drawn up, everything valued and insured, and a specialized warehouse in Buckinghamshire sent a lorry down to pick everything up.

It goes without saying that all this cost me a great deal. In fact, I had to raise money on the equity of my London home. I even paid off the cleaner and got her to mop the floors and dust the rooms before everything was locked up and the key ceremoniously placed in Archie's hand.

She was grateful, and gave me a kiss. On the cheek.

It was a boiling hot day as we set off in the car. Archie was unbuttoned. A bead of sweat in the tiny hollow at the base of her throat burst its banks and moved downwards, coalescing like fat butter on hot toast, then gathering pace, breaking into a gallop as it delightedly found the tightening, shimmering crevice between her orbs.

I fought an insane urge to lean forward and stop its progress with the tip of my tongue. Then I was overwhelmed by disgust. My eyes, moving upwards and alighting upon her right-hand nostril, focused on a long black hair, slightly curled and tipped by a crustaceous nodule of snot.

Some pox, some infectious emotion raged through me. In a mere second the garden had turned rank, somehow. Her skin grew pockmarked. Her breasts swelled in an exaggerated manner, became large shapeless sacks filled with clear aspic, trembling each time the car went over a bump.

Ultimately this distaste that arose in me was a help. I could draw a deep breath and look out the window. Maybe after all I would be able to forget about Archie, or at least relegate her to the second division? Given that she no longer cared for me, would not this be the best thing to do? Or should I pursue her, declare myself? If I did, would she once again transform herself, unfold her body, cleave to me and give me passage?

Ultimately, sexuality dominates us, takes our time and attention away from more important things. And for what? What is woman, after all? Isn't she just a sort of fruit that wanes into a soft, dissipating over-ripeness? Yes. Woman falls into the yellow leaf, in the words of the Bard. Man also has his penance to pay, in the form of castration and loss of erotic powers—only his mozzarella gut is capable of growth. Everything else in slow retreat.

There's a double penalty for man. Post-menopausal woman enters a sort of blissful state of repose, out of which she continues to have full recourse to her sexuality, but man must pay for his sensual transports in blood. He wakes in a cold sweat, ever alert to the test, ever aware of his growing weakness.

In the period that followed our arrival in London, my self-imposed determination to be abstinent—because of my disgust for her—began to change me. My superficial view of Archie evolved from that of a splendidly sexual being, to a chaste and rather annoying incompetent. Was I now seeing Archie as she truly was? Or was it all just a ruse to stop me lusting after her?

In the end I had to concede sex would have been far more satisfying than most other activities we conjured up in the evenings. Sex beats sitting round watching television and eating stale biscuits, which was the sort of thing we usually got up night after night, slumped in my shabby sofa. Archie never seemed to notice the way I constantly and surreptitiously glanced across at her. Disdain or desire—it made no difference to her. Not at all.

All I ever got was the odd pat on the hand, peck on the cheek, and so on.

Question: Bereft of a lover, what is a man?
Answer: A spiritual traveller in search of love.

Man sits on the beach, he sees a beautiful girl, and he is filled with melancholy and regret. He writes "The Girl from Ipanema" but it makes no difference. His lance is broken and only imminent death can free him. For a man, erotic love is all about penetration. Why else did heroes once ride out with their spears to seek out the serpent?

The spear is man's great ally in dealing with the monster.

XIV

Six weeks later I was sitting in my favorite back-street café in Islington with a plate of slop (by that I mean an English breakfast) and a pile of manuscripts in front of me waiting to be read.

Suddenly there was a voice in my ear: "Thought I'd find you here this time of the morning, you old dog." I looked up, and there he was, his usual indomitable self: Jimmy! With a smug grin on his affluent face.

"Jimmy! I didn't know you were in London. You've been keeping your eyes on us?"

"As it happens, yes. I saw your lights on last night."

I put down my newspaper and wiped the chip-grease off my lips. "I'm not much of a dog these days. More of a sheep or something. Wish I was a bloody dog!"

"Don't tell me, she won't fuck you, right?"

"No. She won't."

"Hey! I knew it. But she's taken all your dough. Am I right?"

"A fair chunk, yes."

"Well listen up. I just want you to know there's a membership card waiting for you. My new club, all-male membership, strictly only guys who've been taken round the block by their wives."

"She's not my wife."

"She's living with you."

"Staying! In my spare room."

"And you're paying for her."

"Not really, I just feed her."

"Oh yeah, Little Shop of Horrors, right? Feed me, feed me.

You give her an allowance?"

"Fuck off! You should be giving her an allowance."

"I'd rather make a donation to the fucking Canadian seal cull."

"Look. I know all about it... your erection problems... it's not her fault."

"Excuse me?"

"And your Viagra addiction."

He laughed incredulously. "Oh sure yeah! Ask my new wife. For a guy in his fifties I'm a fucking tiger. I reckon I could jerk off and hit that wall from here. Know what I'm saying?"

I frowned at my manuscripts. "I've got to get through all this. Today."

He grabbed my arm and squeezed it. "Why are you working in this dump? Why aren't you at home?" When I didn't answer straight away he shrieked gleefully. "She asked you to go out, didn't she?"

I hesitated before conceding with a nod. "She's having a few people over for a meditation day."

"Oh fuck!" He whistled. "You're right, you're not a dog. You're not even a fucking sheep, you're dog-meat. You better wake up."

"Maybe I do have to wake up, but I don't need you coming here to gloat at me."

He groaned, "Oh man Chuck, I was just gonna leave you here with your stupid manuscripts and your pain-in-the-ass attitude! I can't believe you helped that bitch get a lawyer and even paid the fees. Are you insane? Where are your loyalties for Christ's sake? I thought we were friends."

I gripped his arm, as if drowning. "Jimmy! I'm in love with her."

Jimmy peeled off my hand. "That's no excuse! I'm your friend! Your goddamn friend! You know what that means to me? It means I can't do it. I can't watch you fuck yourself like this. That's a man you got in there!" he added, with a little punch to my chest. "Remember him? That guy in there who deserves the best, not some bitch using him, depriving him of his rights." He clamped his hand round the back of my neck and gently shook my head. "You don't love her and you never did, you stupid dumb shit! It was something else. It was your issues! Okay? You need a shrink. Have you ever been to see a shrink?"

For weeks I'd had a persistent nervous pain in my solar plexus, and sometimes at night it turned into an agonizing cramp. I suspected it was the beginning of an ulcer. Now, with Jimmy staring at me, I felt it burst into life again. The waitress dropped a huge tray of crockery. There was an almighty crash, followed by scattered applause from the diners, and a fit of roaring from the owner in the kitchen. It was like Jericho falling. I felt my whole life collapsing round me as I gave in to his line of reasoning. Far away I heard Jimmy's eager, weaselling voice working at me: "Talk to me, Klaus! What are you gonna do now?"

"Stop calling me fucking Klaus. You know my fucking name!" I clutched my head, whimpering: "I don't know what I'm going to fucking do! I've got myself into debt. She's glued to my flat. She never leaves, never goes anywhere. And she won't sleep with me. She absolutely refuses."

I noticed he couldn't quite restrain a little smile. "You'll have to give her the flat and hit the road. That's what I did."

There was a moment of transcendent understanding between us.

"Somehow I have to get rid of her," I said at long last.

"You do, you really do. That's your home!"

"Right," I glumly agreed.

"Let's get our asses down the pub and talk this over in detail."

Half an hour later we were comfortably installed in a public house, nibbling at beer nuts and inhaling palls of tobacco smoke.

"I feel bad kicking her out." I sipped at my third pint, still vaguely attracted by the unspoken notion of going home and having a cup of tea with Archie. "She's a human being, not a thing. I can't just get rid of her."

"Everything's a thing, Chuck. What the fuck are you saying? She's an adult—an adult *thing*, okay? That's the operative point. You've got to stick to the point! With women if you don't stick to the point, you're dead!" He spat out each word like a bullet. "You are not obliged to spend time with her. It's this thing about owing people, this guilt trip you're on, you've gotta work on that. That's where a shrink could help you out. I mean in the end who are you gonna please? Yourself or everyone else?"

"Sometimes when people feel guilty it's because they've actually done something wrong."

"You sorry little Catholic!"

"Archie's got nowhere to go."

Jimmy shook his head confidently. "She's got friends, contacts and money."

"She doesn't have a penny!"

"That's what she tells you. The first thing you've got to realize is Archie's rich. Damn sight richer than you."

"How do you figure that?"

"I gave her a damned house that's gotta be worth a million euro at least. She's got no debts. She can sell that and retire. She's got all the documentation, can go down to the bank and borrow twenty thousand bucks against that piece of property without any problem at all, then lease herself a place in like Chelsea until she's set up. It wouldn't take her long to find some guy with money. Okay, Chuck?" He reached out and grabbed my neck again in that good old American way of his. "Okay? We're not all like you. We're not all little guys running around trying to be nice to everyone. Okay?"

"Okay what, Jimmy? What's okay? I have a woman at home that I've spent a hell of a lot of energy and time trying to help. She needed it. She was defenceless. I picked her up off the ground."

He laughed. "Archie defenseless? Give me a break. She's like a bloody quarterback."

"Why am I even talking to you? I'm being disloyal. I'm

deserting her."

"You are, Jimmy. You are deserting her. And she deserves it."

"I'll miss her when she goes."

"For a couple of weeks. Then you'll be ecstatic to have your life back. Maybe you'll even find a new woman."

I thought about Archie in bed, with her pale blue bedside lamp, the cups of herbal tea teetering on the edge. I thought about Archie in her silk negligee, frowning as she lay there reading a self-help book.

"You've got to take the medicine, Chuck! You've got to stop this creepy stuff. You can't feel guilty about kicking someone out who's basically a parasite. You get me? What are you, some kind of saint? Find yourself a woman who brings home a nice piece of damn meat now and then and cooks you a meal, then takes off her clothes and fucks you."

"You're just a capitalist, Jimmy, and everything's about what you want for yourself."

"Just listen to yourself. You're so scared of standing up for what you actually want! Yes, I'm a capitalist about the things I want. And to be honest, if you could just stop being the nice guy for one minute, I reckon you would be too."

XV

Jimmy's plan, and by inference, mine, was as follows:

I would go back to the flat, tell Archie that as a surprise I'd booked a weekend getaway at a country hotel. Once we had left, Jimmy would let himself in with the spare key and pack her things. These he would arrange to have delivered to the country hotel where, as a gesture of tax-deductible largesse, Archie would be booked in to stay for a week. According to Jimmy this was time enough for her to "figure out" where she was going next.

Meanwhile, Jimmy would arrange for a locksmith to change the front door locks. I would already have a key for the new lock.

If anything went wrong and Archie bolted back to London, she wouldn't be able to get back into the flat.

On Saturday night I would leave a note for her, explaining my reasons, and then simply drive back to London without her.

That last bit seemed cowardly but Jimmy said if I actually told her face-to-face of my decision, I would definitely fold. Archie would overpower me with her feminine wiles, and I wouldn't be able to follow through.

I wouldn't go back to the flat for at least two weeks. Jimmy reasoned, probably correctly, that if she came knocking on the door, I'd simply let her in.

In practice, this is how it happened:

As I walked into the flat after our lengthy drinking session, I smelt perfume and heard Edith Piaf from her bedroom. I knocked and walked in. Archie was lying in bed, reading. She smiled. "You're drunk, naughty boy. Did you finish the manuscripts?"

"No. How was the meditation session?"

"In the end we were all too tired. We're doing it tomorrow."

"I can just go back to the café." I perched on the edge of the bed, unsure about setting the plan in motion. "Archie?"

I stared at her for a while, as I actually didn't know what to say. Then in the end I remembered there was something else I'd always wanted to ask her. "Did you really have an abortion? I need to know."

"No," she said. "I didn't. I don't know why I told you that. I think I wanted you to feel sorry for me. Actually I hardly even had sex with Bertie. Only once, at the ashram, which didn't mean very much as we were supposed to have sex with people there, particularly old ugly people we weren't the least bit attracted to. That's why I left." She looked at me. "Does that answer your question?"

"Yes." I squirmed. "Archie, I've arranged a little surprise for us. A weekend away. I found a little country house hotel in

Gloucestershire. Looks lovely."

She sat up abruptly, stared at me. "You've been talking to Jimmy!"

"What?"

"It would never even occur to you to pay for a weekend break."

"What can you mean?"

"Jimmy was obsessed with country house hotels. It was practically the only thing he ever thought about. Going to Gloucestershire and ordering himself a rack of lamb and pouring fifteen Tia Marias down his throat with me as his prisoner in some god-awful Jacobean mansion!" She stopped and shuddered, glaring at me, a tiny twist of smoke (to my mind, at least) rising from her nostrils. "God Chuck, I can't believe you've gone behind my back like this, talking to him! After all we've been through! I thought you were on my side."

I started back-pedaling like mad. "I... he... thought... just... that you should maybe be more... give more time for me to... sort out some space issues here..." I said.

"He thought I was using you?"

"Well—"

"In a way I have been using you, Chuck, and I'm sorry. I thought you were big enough to carry me for a while. Obviously I was wrong."

She jumped out of bed, full of energy. She wrenched off her nightgown and stood in front of me. "Take a good look," she said, "you won't be seeing this again." Her weeks in London had transformed her. Why are women so good at transformation? She was wearing a pair of sheer pink knickers that hugged her buttocks deliciously. I felt a swelling, tortuous erection, the product of months of abstinence.

She stopped and looked at me. "And to think I was actually thinking of sleeping with you again."

As cruelty goes, that one really hit the spot. I felt like I'd been shot, or rather, I wished someone would shoot me. I watched her getting dressed, like a forlorn hitchhiker as a car speeds past and disappears.

"Archie, I'm sorry."

"It's too late. I know you're sorry. Thanks for being sorry, thanks for all you've done for me."

She carried on packing.

"I didn't think. I didn't know. I wasn't thinking, I just felt there was something which, if it could be done, then we'd be..."

"You don't know what you think. That's the problem. Chuck, darling, I told you that when we first met, do you remember?"

I didn't remember.

She continued rifling through her underwear drawer, pulling out delicious lingerie, some of which I recognized from those intoxicating weeks in Sardinia. I realized how stupid I'd been. I absolutely adored her! To think I'd even tried to convince myself I found her physically repulsive! How much self-deception was it possible for a man to load himself with? I was like a fucking donkey with a pair of tits hanging in front of my face!

"I forgive you. Don't worry, I won't think badly of you." She continued packing hurriedly, and refused my help in getting the suitcase down the stairs. "I'll send someone for the rest!" she called from below on her way out.

When the door closed there was a moment of utter silence. With ponderous steps I walked up to the door and locked it. Then I went to my hi-fi cabinet and searched through my CD collection until I found what I was looking for: Rimsky-Korsakov's "Scheherazade."

I felt quite blissful as those first few haunting bars filled the room. Then, sinking onto the couch, I promptly burst into tears.

XVI

Something about that drunken afternoon in the pub and the excruciating final curtain in my flat never quite left me.

Jimmy's words had a profound effect on me, even though I

believe him to be the most wickedly misogynistic man I have ever met. It was, I believe, the first time in my whole life that I'd been genuinely changed by something said to me. Because I acted on it. That's the operative point. Once you act, all hell breaks loose. Dithering, which is my usual way, makes other people believe they can tell you what to do. They can, and they will, if you let them.

After Archie left, I spent some time licking my wounds.

Then I woke up to my life. My autumnal life, all covered in ivy.

I took early retirement, sold my flat and emigrated. Crazy as it sounds, I moved to Rio de Janeiro, where I now live. I run a small business which never fails to turn a profit. Alongside my pension and my cash pile from selling up in London, this means that for the first time in my life I am affluent.

Every morning when I wake up I look at my wife, a bright, beautiful Brazilian in her thirties who positively bubbles with joie de vivre within minutes of waking up.

The thing I most love about her is that she has no ambition at all except to be happy. And in this respect she is my perfect mirror-image. We drink coffee, we have lunch, we go dancing. I'm learning the samba. We sit on the terrace in the evenings over tête-à-tête dinners, then we go to the cinema. In the summer, which is practically the whole year, we go to a beach house she has up the coast. We swim and throw parties for a myriad of friends, all of whom adore me (as I "adore" them) and call me Jacques because no one can say Chuck.

I don't miss Chuck at all.

I am fifty-one, but my life has only just started. I'm conserving my energy and keeping fit. My wife wants three children.

Sometimes I wake in the night. I lie there listening to my wife's breathing. It's a reassuring sound. On certain nights I can also hear the surf coming in. I know I could not be a happier man. Yet I often think of Archie and her heroic madness. In spite of her confusion, it was Archie who saved me.

We need the mad people to help us break through the barriers, even though, once they disappear, they leave us tainted. Our love for them cannot be eradicated. It flourishes in the ground like wild garlic, and when the nights are still, there's a lingering scent.

People set off in life expecting bright, breathless dawns, followed by reflective, calm sunsets. They shouldn't expect things to run smooth. They shouldn't expect their hearts to be spared. Why? My conclusion may seem simplistic, but nonetheless, here it is:

Love doesn't work!

My Gift, My Dictation

Life is a rare mystery. When we look beyond our lives, we see only darkness. If we could turn time on its head and go back to the time before we were born, we would see a commensurate darkness there too. Beginnings hold an even greater mystery than endings, for death can only exist when preceded by life. Yet surely the first and the last darkness is the same?

For that reason, whenever I go to a funeral, I spare a thought for all those who have never been born, those who—whether by coincidence or misfortune—will never win the lottery of birth.

I should also add that the only thing of any importance is the short flash of light in which we, the momentary owners of an ordered mass of atomic substance, are free to express ourselves through language. Life is like a planet, an island, an albatross riding its fixed trade winds. On this speck of rock lives a people besieged by its own lack of understanding, a people of brutish sensibility, a people of thunderous ignorance. Surrounded by an army of mistaken notions, we skulk in our citadel and wage our lonely struggles against insanity and starvation.

As a young man I found a marked tendency in the humanoid species to talk nonsense and do ridiculous things. Therefore at the age of thirty-eight I decided to take control of the world and impose systematic reform. Now that I am approaching a grand old age of ninety and face my own journey into darkness, I will set out some thoughts so that those who follow in my enormous footsteps may understand my reasoning in all that I have done.

What follows are some brief notes on the fifty years that I have held the human race under the sway of my dictatorship.

The instrument of my mastery, if you will, was that I invented a way of atomizing anyone who resisted me. When I say invented, I mean that I discovered an inner capability that effectively rendered me a god. What human could ever defeat a world leader who, on the merest whim, could disband the atoms in any given body and turn it to vapor?

Furthermore, I was capable of reading people's minds. Hence conspirators were rooted out as a matter of course.

My rise to power was inexorable. I quickly removed a host of figures invoking liberty and democracy and raising armies to fight me in the name of high ideals. It took me no more than a morning's work to rid the world of my opponents.

It may seem sadistic to admit to these things, but I remember rather enjoying the unceremonious removal of the world's political leaders. I particularly enjoyed breaking up a veritable legion of freemasons and other morbid, secret societies, whose members often included some of the most powerful and the most childish people in the world.

I recall many impassioned speeches by these rhetorical

hooligans. I made a habit of visiting parliaments and civic halls in every country. There I would sit in the speaker's chair and listen as orators stood up and spoke about the torch of liberty passing from one generation to the next. I wanted to give them a chance to absolve themselves. As a philosophical ruler, I always had to understand the arguments of my opponents.

Afterwards, I patiently explained to them that they must not fear the darkness that I would soon impose upon them. Life is an utter illusion, and whether we face the darkness today or in thirty years makes precious little difference.

Oh, but how pitiful the arguments were. Societies in those days were ruled by high principles, while practical day-to-day life was brutish and deeply immoral. Presidents and prime ministers excused themselves from true responsibility by declaring themselves mere custodians of their positions of power. They were not free to act outside the rule of law. The judiciaries of these same societies would similarly declare that they were not empowered to change the law unless so instructed by higher powers.

The main thing going wrong in those times was the notion that individuals were entitled to things, anything they could buy. This was known as economic liberalism. People worked so that they could buy things they wanted: houses, cars, clothes, holidays, jewelry and other fripperies. Among the less intelligent, and by that I mean the vast majority, rich men attracted beautiful women, and vice-versa. The yardstick of human worth for a woman was beauty, and for a man, wealth.

I took the opposite view. It seemed to me that people were not entitled to anything. They had to learn to be grateful for anything they had, particularly consciousness, which is a marvelous gift.

People's desires had begun to transcend the world itself. Millions of tiny proles were driving about in filthy cars, spewing out various gases that began to throw the planetary climate system into imbalance. The universities were full to bursting with ignorant youths. Every year these sickly little shoots were released to proliferate like noxious weeds. And before long half of them were dreaming of sitting at tables with sea-views in Monte Carlo, while their super-yachts weltered on the waves below. In the poorer parts of the world, meanwhile, people wanted exactly the same things. They struggled to send their children to the very same universities, so that they would also be able to buy the useless plastic electronic junk that their wealthy northern brethren so coveted.

Then there were some smaller groups of native peoples who still clung on to decent beliefs. But they, along with what remained of the planet's stock of wild animals, had mostly been wiped out, stuffed and exhibited in ethnography museums. Their land had been turned over to something hideous, a process which in those days went by the name of development.

As soon as I took power, I abolished a number of things that seemed to me unhelpful to the future world order I had in mind. These included cars, aircraft, cameras, refrigerators, computers, radios, fixed line and mobile telephony, and so on. Small numbers of these same objects were still manufactured, but I stipulated that at least fifty percent of their components had to be handmade. This had two immediate effects: an enormous upsurge in craftsmanship, and huge price increases, making such consumer articles unaffordable to more or less everyone. Human health improved enormously, as people took to walking, cycling and riding horses.

I was not a backward dictator. I built telephone exchanges in every town and village. Many objects could be hired at reasonable cost, and hospitals and schools were equipped with all the high technology the human race was capable of.

The Internet struck me as a tool ideal for the spread of filth and corruption, so I abolished it. I quickly rooted out its criminals, pornographers and profiteers and turned them to gas.

Music has always struck me as the noblest of all arts, but I felt the distribution of recorded music had deeply damaged its fabric. Hence I prohibited the sale of all CDs and vinyl, and built concert halls and smaller venues all over the countries of the world, where people were free to play their instruments.

The travel industry was disbanded. I felt it important that people should be able to travel if they so chose, but I wanted a return to the parochialism that had ruled the world up until the early 1800s. In those days any journey across national boundaries was hazardous, as packs of wolves attacked carriages, and a lack of hotels and restaurants made travel something for the hardy. Also, travelers then actually had something to report upon. The foods of foreign lands, the languages and customs of distant climes, were notable and unique. Prior to the revolution, I was saddened by the globalization that the world's cretinous leaders seemed to feel was such a noble thing. Their weird and twisted manipulation of natural economics caused enormous numbers of people to migrate hither and thither in search of prosperity. I emphasize that this transmigration had nothing to do with the poverty of the lands these people left behind. Many a time a family would set out, leaving a pleasant green valley behind where their forefathers had farmed for many millennia, choosing instead some vast, filthy city with the prospect of soulless work in laundries, restaurants or other places that did not merit existence. Languages had begun to shrink and disappear. Habits and customs were merging everywhere and people no longer knew who they were. This was all excused in the name of multiculturalism, as it was known in the richer countries. In fact, the intellectuals of these countries conveniently excused the fact that the poor peoples of the world were their slaves, living in the nastiest, filthiest areas and doing the jobs no one with any self-respect would ever touch. To compound this misery, this same intellectual ruler class soon emigrated with its pots of money into the overpopulated poorer countries, buying up vast tracts of land and further enslaving the peasants. Soon, the poor countries were full of spa resorts and luxury hotels. Within another half a century, the so-called third world had also become a market for all of the cheap, mass-produced electronics and motorcars so prized by the capitalists.

It was more or less at this time that I stepped in.

I have become the most hated man in the history of the human race. I have not sought to defend myself, because it matters little to me what people think. In my own heart I know that I have been the savior of the planet.

Some of my reforms were unpopular. I allowed the sea to reclaim large tracts of land in Holland and Bangladesh and other low-lying land. I have always been fond of the sea, and there is no good argument for devoting enormous resources to holding it back from its rightful sphere of influence. To restore Neptune's kingdom, I stopped all coastal and ocean fisheries for a period of twenty-five years. My critics, none of whom survived, pointed out that this would cause hardship and starvation. This never occurred, because in the same period the global population was considerably reduced. In fact, I found it necessary to atomize the genitalia of about ninety percent of the population. Within forty years this had the desired effect without, I think you will agree, any excessive cruelty. The freedom to have sex struck me, then as now, as highly debatable. At the beginning of my reign, I felt that people had become over-sexualized. Hence I decided that sex should be raised to the level of art. I encouraged an open presentation of sex as a part of the sacred ritual of life. However, like many mystics before me, I struggled to control my own response to eroticism, and finally came to the conclusion that only by atomizing my own genitalia could I remain impartial. This was swiftly done and I have never regretted it.

Of course I also screened people who would have the responsibility of producing tomorrow's children. In my earlier days it had always troubled me that the vulgar mob—particularly alcoholics, psychopaths and other regressives—produced the majority of the children, who quickly followed in their parents' ravaged footsteps, mainly because the intricacies of contraception were beyond their minuscule comprehensions.

People wanting children had to apply for Child Seeker's Permits, which were only ever awarded after a lengthy consultative process.

I also immediately reduced the size of the world's megacities by about 75 percent. My method was severe, but in my view fair. I would walk through cities and retain buildings that struck me as having some kind of architectural worth. All other buildings I atomized, and in their place established parks or dwellings. Of course, taste played a part here. Some may question whether one man's subjective view should have had such free rein. But they would be democrats, and democrats do not understand the nature of solving problems. Democrats merely believe in the sacred necessity of discussing problems until those problems grow out of control.

Any buildings that had been built for profit, without any thought for the aesthetic consequences, were simply removed.

Economically, my reforms were not immediately a success, and after a global economic slump I responded by abolishing all currencies and replacing them with nothing.

Food, clothing, and housing were free. Everything else was paid for in work. Work was itself a currency, and those who refused to work were simply atomized. Sick and elderly people were permitted to live in hospitals for a certain amount of time, but if their friends or families were unwilling to care for them, they were eventually atomized in a place of their choosing. At first, societies found this a cruel practice, but as people came to accept the constant presence of the darkness outside this globule we call life, they gradually began to defer to its power. The darkness becomes less pervasive once we choose the time of our meeting with it. It was the haphazard nature of death that caused humans to fear it.

Religion was a thorny problem. I have always viewed religion as a good distraction from the business of life. Life, and all matter, is deeply corrupt. Religion, by its very nature, is evanescent and removed from the vagaries of physical life. It is one of the few areas where idealism may be justified. Hence I built monasteries, churches, mosques and temples. I allowed people to pursue their religions. Several religious orders set up hospitals and other places of refuge for sick and ailing people. My one stipulation was that the religious were not allowed to speak of their faith. Debates were to be conducted in writing only. This led to a renaissance in the art of writing. Extremists or martyrs were atomized before they had time to hoist their flags and holler the name of some tainted theology. Their fervent cries gurgled in their throats as they crumbled into stray atoms.

I have always been a believer in brevity, and although I have been an absolute ruler for a half century, I do not hold myself so important that I shall leave long accounts of my life, as so many others have done. Julius Caesar, for instance. Hence I have destroyed all of my belongings, including books, letters, and other personal effects. The only thing I shall leave behind is a small necklace of white gold set with a single topaz. This, to remind those who come after me that the human home is a realm of pure refracted light. We must not believe in the ultimate value of the individual, for the individual is nothing but a base collection of desires and vanities.

Some may believe that I have been a harsh man, imposing himself on the earth. To these people, who after my passing will be free to criticize me, I only wish to say this: history is full of mad dictators who have killed mindlessly. Had I been such a man, the earth would not be here today.

I have no doubt that within a few years of my death, humanity will resume its reckless charge towards self-destruction. But I do not have eternal life, nor would I wish to spend an eternity restraining an infant child from stumbling towards the edge of a cliff.

I see no further reason to prevent this child falling into the immense glittering sea that lies below. It is my view that if the infant wishes to fall, then at least let him fall in beauty, like the Greek charioteer.

I hope that, in my absence, we shall at least accomplish this.

Gradisca

i) Prologue

Now I must tell you about Gradisca. *Gradisca*! Embodiment of my failure, also my separation from what I have always sought.

For the sake of simplicity, let's just call it happiness.

Where do I begin? How can I describe the choices I made? I, who do not even believe in the idea of choice, this erroneous concept invented by neo-liberal economists.

Most of us can do nothing but accept the path laid out for us.

We do not steer the ship. We are towed in its wake.

The Greeks knew the gods do not often take humans for their lovers, but Gradisca was bound to be discovered soon by an Olympian, then quickly and efficiently spirited away. I wonder if she knew this grand thing she had become in my eyes? I suspect not. Like all magical beings, she seemed unaware of her own significance.

Gradisca: I see her in my mind like a naiad, wearing a green knitted top that finished just below her navel and perfect jeans, sculpted to her hips. At the approach of midday she stands as always in the window of her watch shop, her face tastefully and lightly made up, those slight wrinkles at the corners of her eyes indicative of the fact that she is a woman in her late thirties. Every day she's on duty behind her counter, except in the summer, when she's often outside on the pavement. She likes the taste of freedom, holding spirited conversations on her mobile or chatting to passing acquaintances.

Once I saw a group of pubescent boys, crammed into a dilapidated car with speed stripes, slamming on their brakes when they saw her, to ask for directions. Gradisca was happy to oblige.

In the summer months she goes religiously to the ice cream bar twice a day. The mirrors are always kept polished there, it is the perfect place to touch up one's hair and make-up. Or maybe she just liked ice cream? Sometimes I was in the ice cream bar having coffee or a grappa when she walked in. In fact, thinking about it, it only happened once or twice.

There was too much electricity between Gradisca and me. I knew that if I ever touched her there would be no way back for me. This was not an option.

I have a complicating factor. I'm married. Nominally married, you could say. My wife lives far away. I haven't seen her in a very long while. From time to time she writes, tells me how much she misses me. And of course I get sent her bills, which I have to pay.

It's not a very satisfactory arrangement.

Nonetheless, looking back, I suppose it was easier to avoid the Gradisca conundrum altogether, keeping her as a fantasy. Why rip the chest cavity open, why expose the pump?

The first time I went to the watch shop, I was with my father. He was enquiring about an alarm clock, and Gradisca was facing him squarely with a charmed smile on her face.

That day my father was wearing a slightly old-fashioned but ironed and neat-looking checkered cotton shirt. As usual, he was clean-shaven and suave as he took off his sunglasses and waved his hand slightly in the air, launching into his mellifluous Italian. He kept his chin down and looked slightly pressurized.

We said goodbye, and I noted that Gradisca pointedly included me in her polite farewell even though I hadn't spoken to her.

She was wearing a wrap-around blouse of a type I've never seen before. It clutched the outline of her breasts with a deep-plunging hem, and yet it revealed absolutely nothing. Infinitely sexy, utterly sophisticated. Few women can dress like that. I don't think I will ever forget the way she looked that day.

As we walked out, I realized I had been pole-axed.

"I had to concentrate in there," admitted my father, who is almost seventy years old.

I was by myself the second time I went into Gradisca's shop, probably no more than a week later. I wanted to see whether this woman was really as stratospheric as all that.

Or had it been a trick of the light?

When I walked in, my first emotion was disappointment: she was not wearing the famous wrap-around blouse. She had an Indian cotton skirt on, red as blood, and a body-hugging green top that matched her eyes. Her skin glowed like dark African honey. She must have been spending time on the beach.

Again, she gave me a friendly reception, smiling encouragingly as I tried to speak Italian. I asked her to check the battery in my watch. As she rummaged in a drawer, I analyzed her discreet yet also suggestive cleavage, but not for long enough to risk being caught out. I kept myself correct, paid and left.

A few days later I saw her walking in the main piazza, where some young boys kicking a ball stopped and looked as she passed by. I followed at a discreet distance, admiring those small feet and shapely calves, that rounded posterior of substance, the long chestnut brown hair that rippled with vitality against her shoulder-blades.

As I stared, I sensed many other eyes pursuing her. A hushed silence had fallen over everything. Everyone watched as she traversed the bleached sunlit piazza with quickening steps, desperate to get off the public stage.

A thought hit me. Maybe it was significant that she worked in a watch shop? In some way my feelings for Gradisca related to time, its passage.

All my life was about waiting, waiting for a wife who never came home.

Gradisca, in her shop of pendulums and chimes.

Gradisca, peering at her watch, waiting to go home.

Gradisca, herself a time-piece, a woman most likely longing for a child before it was too late.

With Gradisca there was an opportunity to halt the passing of time. To live, instead. To be in the moment and never again have to be out of step. A form of immortality, almost.

The third time I went in to see Gradisca I felt she was prepared for me. As soon as I entered the pristine shop with its expansive, polished marble floors, as soon as I slid across the floor towards a revolving plastic tower of sunglasses, she made her way over to me.

Not eagerly, exactly, but attentively.

There was something sluggish about me, as if time was dragging indecently at my capacity to speak. I managed to say in very poor Italian that my eyes were hurting. I needed some shades. She nodded and indicated I should sit down. Then she faced me squarely, gazing thoughtfully at my face before gently removing my glasses.

"These!" she said, carefully slotting a pair of futuristic frames into position.

I looked at myself in the mirror, twisting and turning and wishing I could suavely whip out some cash and buy them. But they weren't me, to be honest, nor did I have very much cash. In the end, I simply put my old, scratched glasses back on and told her what I really needed was a new watch. My old Japanese model was unreliable.

She crossed the marble floor and slid open a drawer, picked up a wristwatch and dangling it in the air for me to see; then gestured for me to come and have a look.

But I shook my head, overwhelmed by my inability to speak in a language she could understand. My mind was bursting with little comments, jokes, remarks I would have liked to tell her. Instead, all I had was my large, ungainly body and my empty hands.

"No. Grazie."

There was a hollow silence, a silence that seemed to cry out for something to be said, so she politely asked: "Qualcos'altro?"

I shook my head and started backing away. I was just about to turn round when she launched a smile that punctured and passed clean through my ventricles.

The intricate expressiveness of that smile overwhelmed me. First, this was certainly some attempt on her part to communicate despite our verbal differences. I felt she was aware of our communication problems, hence she had to try and say something with her smile. And she certainly had. With that smile she told me everything.

Of course it could only have been in my mind. Our eyes must have met for a mere fraction of a second. Then I walked out. I was boiling with desire, but the lava was bubbling far below the surface, and there was a thick plug of rock on top.

One day I would blow up.

Later that day I was in the ice cream bar talking to Rafaela, my landlady, a pleasant-looking woman in her late forties with large crystal earrings, untidy hair, Birkenstocks, always with a selection of crap drawings she tried to sell you. At a quarter to five, fifteen minutes before the shop was opening, Gradisca sauntered in. At first she didn't see me. I was talking to Rafaela, discussing something fairly practical, like a faulty water meter or similar, but I was unable to take my eyes off the other side of the bar, where Gradisca was performing a sort of dance, by which I mean she was whirling in front of the mirror, buffing her hair and making sure her tight-fitting t-shirt looked right. Now and then she would look over at the girl at the counter, making some joke or casual remark. The two of them seemed more than close, almost like members of the same family.

From time to time she lifted her eyes and glanced in my direction with enormous intensity. I noticed because I could see her reflection in the mirror and I was able to study her face as she was watching me. Even more unexpectedly, she kept glancing nervously at Rafaela. Perhaps wondering who this rival might be?

I was vaguely aware of Rafaela saying things to me, but I was in another world. Gradisca left the mirror and walked out, passing close to where we were standing. We smiled at each other. "Bona sera," I said.

She looked relieved and reciprocated.

In the next few days I just occasionally glanced through the windows as I passed. Sometimes I saw her standing there. On one occasion I passed just as she was bending forward to pick something up. Her rump was towards the window. I couldn't avoid feasting my eyes.

The fourth time I entered her shop was important. I had a sense of wanting to achieve something that fourth time. I had some vague idea of asking her for dinner, or a drink. Where, though? There weren't any restaurants around. And what bars did she like?

Or might I cook for her?

The day before, I had seen her strolling down the Corso, occasionally glancing into shop windows, moving towards me from about a hundred meters away. I stared at the ground to avoid catching her eye, thinking to myself that as we got closer I would look up and smile at her. Then I'd stop and try to start up a conversation.

Ten seconds passed, then I looked up.

She'd gone!

At first I was disappointed. I realized she must have gone into a shop.

Then it occurred to me that she had probably wanted to avoid me. But why? A whole range of possibilities arose in my mind. Was she being elusive to enflame me and test my mettle?

Another thought occurred to me. Maybe she didn't know what to say to me, just as I didn't to her?

In either case, now I knew she was aware of my presence. I wasn't just someone with a burning interest in wristwatches.

So, as I was saying, the fourth visit was significant, because now we both knew that there was something in the air. As I walked across the cool stone tiles, she was watching me with a tentative smile. She had a slight edge to her. I felt she was expecting me to do or say something. I lost my nerve and stood before her, uncomfortable in my own body. I seemed incapable of lightness in her presence.

Finally, at a loss, I asked for a cheap quartz watch with a rubber strap. Even my voice seemed to have lost its normal timbre. When I was paying I noticed my hand was trembling. I took fractionally too long getting my money out and when I slotted the wallet into my inside pocket I got it caught in the frayed silk lining.

She seemed to be watching my every move. There was a kind of weariness about her, and I realized I had overstepped the mark in some way. Not by saying anything, not even really by doing anything. Just by being. By existing in her presence I had made her weary.

I said goodbye and left. Later that day I bumped into her

again in the street and she quite blatantly dived into a souvenir shop to avoid me when I was only some ten meters in front of her. I walked past and told myself it was now crystal clear why she had been avoiding me. She didn't like me, found me unpleasant and heavy-footed with my poor command of Italian, my awkward northern manners. It was an embarrassment, this fawning passion I had developed for her. I decided never to bother her again, and never to go into the watch shop again.

That would have been the end of the story, except there were some other convolutions. First, I met her sister, because she started working in the ice cream bar. I didn't know for sure if she was Gradisca's sister, and I didn't ask. But they looked the same. The sister was like her twin, except she looked older. I had a feeling she was married and more settled. Every day a guy in a vintage roadster picked her up.

It was a two-seater, so I never saw Gradisca get a lift with them.

I never saw Gradisca with anyone. Only when she was working in the shop was she actually with someone else. Sometimes I saw her talking to people in the street, but I always had the impression they were acquaintances to meet for an aperitif.

Never a man, holding her possessively.

Gradisca's sister had more solidity about her. She wasn't ethereal. Beauty must have been a family trait, but even though she looked more matronly I fancied she was actually younger than Gradisca.

Oddly enough, I found the sister very easy to talk to. Not like Gradisca at all. She had a basic command of English; I made jokes and we had some half-reasonable times in there, just talking about ice cream or how to mix drinks or what sort of cakes we liked with our coffee.

One day while we were talking it hit me! Jesus, what an idiot I had been.

Gradisca had a boyfriend. Obviously!

A girl like that, poised and well groomed and gorgeous

with it. Of course! How could I have ignored this most obvious explanation of all?

My speculation didn't lead anywhere, until one day after too many drinks I told a friend I had developed a crush on a woman in town.

"Tell me who?" he said, interrupting me with a delighted grin.

"She works in a shop."

"Which one?"

"The watch shop."

He chuckled. "Gradisca? Excellent!"

"Go on!"

"Everyone likes her, and she knows it."

I told him about our trysts in the shop, how I felt there was something between us, then my puzzlement about the way she had avoided me in the street.

"You can't just expect a woman to stop and talk to you in the street, can you? You don't even know her. Anyway, Gradisca's a bit of a special case. And she has a boyfriend."

"Aha! That's what I thought."

"A boring fat doctor. No one can understand what she's doing with him. Maybe she likes the money? But I also hear they're just about to split up."

"So she's famous in town?"

"Everyone's famous, even you," he said. "People notice everything you do here. Gradisca used to be married, I know that. It didn't work and she came back. I don't have much detail on that, though."

He paused then shook his head and smiled. "Today I saw her wearing this green knitwear thing that reached down to her navel more or less, and her lovely big ass was kind of screaming. She's everyone's fantasy but she's in her own world. Like she's playing a game. She comes into our bar sometimes, stands there having a drink and wiggling what she's got, then leaves without saying much. I never go into her shop, though. My wife knows I have a thing about Gradisca, I've told her, there's no point denying it. Everyone's got a thing about Gradisca."

"So what does she get out of it? Going to your bar like that?"

"It's a kind of theatre. Like the struggle between us."

"Who?"

"Boys, girls. The battle."

Later, walking home, it occurred to me that his words were a sort of distortion. Not in their essential points of fact: I believed that Gradisca had been married, otherwise it would not make sense, anything about her. I believed that she had come back in disgrace. The other stuff about her looking for attention, being a cockteaser, struck me as off-the-point and also untrue. Gradisca had grace! All she'd done was walk into a bar! The truth was, I felt admiration for her, the way my friend had described her standing there, confronting the builders, the drinkers and shepherds.

In a way, she was saying to them: "Go home, toss off in your rooms, do what the hell you like, I can stand here, I can do anything I want, and if you desire me that's not my problem." I tried to imagine how it would feel to be a fantasy. Walking round, having all these women looking at me dreamily, eyeing up my bulging crotch, then coming up to ask for directions, smiling appreciatively at my every word.

No wonder Gradisca had turned slightly tricky. If everyone I met desired me, I would find it hard to choose. Not choosing anyone would be the most likely scenario. I would keep myself to myself. Or perhaps I would turn into a player, a fleshpot, always finding new women to distract myself with: tall, small-titted Cuban dancers, pallid Chinese women with shining tresses of jet-black hair.

When would my search ever end?

Oddly enough I think it would end the day I met Gradisca and we spent our nights close together with nothing between us but a film of sweat; and our evenings after she came home from work sitting on my terrace, eating melon and drinking Campari sodas.

ii) Gradisca's Shadow

> *"...there is another side to the Don Juan character which is found in the fused Hebrew-Arabic-Castilian philosophy and concept of reality. This concept is simply that exterior reality has no existence in and of itself. One reaches toward it, and it recedes... Don Juan, thus, somewhat like the wandering Spanish pìcaro, clutches again and again at a phantom. In his case it is the phantom of femininity..."*
> *(John Armstrong Crow, "Spain, the Root and the Flower")*

I

What is Gradisca's shadow? It seems to have a life all of its own. An obscure Christian veil? Or guilt, obsession?

Every moment in our lives represents some choice that will affect everything.

Jung was right. We move through a world of mythical significance.

Behind every beautiful woman you desire, comes a question: Why?

After she has gone, you dwell in the footsteps she left behind. You compose songs on the shore, in honor of Urania who sailed away.

II

Sexual love is love, but love is only love if it is for The One, and by that I mean the beloved object.

The Platonic Love Ideal is an invention designed to focus the mind on the possibilities of Monotheistic Worship. The tribes of Judea invented the One God. In a universe inhabited by One Great Holy Ghost, Man would also have to find the One Beloved Woman (Object as Non-Object) and claim her by a ring on her finger.

The Greek Gods, each a facet of the Jungian diamond, receded. Men would no longer explore the variegations of the feminine serpent, nor the cloven-hoofed Satyr.

III

Beauty/sex is a shadow, because it promises something that is incomplete. Beauty/sex is only a beginning, a door. Men who follow it are men who prefer to loiter on the outside.

When men are young they set out and see the world. Later, when they are older they must cast illusion aside.

"Beauty" is one such illusion.

As men grow older and acquire wisdom, which is after their fortieth year, they should be thinking of their woman and bride. They should spend much of their time in mountains. They should exert themselves greatly for the good of their house.

When I see a beautiful woman I feel pity for her.

IV

Sexual ecstasy is a veil. If you pursue it, know this at least, that it will lead you away from the pursuit of the One God and the One Love.

Life, as we all know, is decrepitude and descent into death.

Sexual desire is like a sail made of sweet-wrappers. It will not perform, but its making was sweet.

V

Hamlet was right, there is no better thing than lying between maiden thighs.

I listen to the maiden's fluting voice whilst moonlight falls upon a bunch of dried flowers.

VI

I have never seen a forty-three-year-old man who is happy and constantly pursuing young beautiful women, unless he is a man of the world, concerned with matter and ownership and the outward shape of things.

Such a man will be satisfied as long as he gets the grand prize, a small clam situated in the region of the crotch. In return he will offer his local delicacy, a sausage-like thing with mayonnaise coming out the end.

VII

I am standing on a hill. Snow is falling, settling on my shoulders.

I see myself as extraneous in the human universe. Sometimes I wonder if I am not already living in a society that has dissolved? Insurance companies and banks send me letters, all inconsequential crap. I rip them into small pieces and put them in my painted waste paper basket from Rajasthan.

The world is full of Freudians. God damn the Freudians, with their dumb goatee beards like pig's bristle on their weak chins.

I am a Jungian, standing on a hill, with frost settling on my shoulders. The fields are barren. I am barren too.

VIII

Could it be that there is some sort of shadow moving across my world, my life? Am I intrinsically flawed—a man with a design fault? Why, when things are in front of me, do I turn away, disdain them? I have turned my life into a struggle against rules I have imposed to bind myself?

IX

What does One Love mean?

Is it anything but idealization, the Love Object surrounded by dark shadows?

Have I chosen to live in One Love surrounded by encroaching shadows?

X

If I could kiss Gradisca's lips today, if I could thrust myself into her innermost womb and expend myself there, would she turn into One Love? No, because One Love is invented myth. Most myths are spontaneous, true, and demotic. One Love does not keep company with other myths; it feeds on fatty, unwholesome soup. Its object is unreality.

XI

Everything is illusion. Life has no real meaning.

Heaven is a place invented by people too lazy to make their own.

I am sure there is no heaven except when I am lying in the arms of my darling, and tonight she is so very far away. It makes me feel alone.

I'm so fucking stoned I could die.

iii) The Night of San Giorgio

Earlier, the streets had been packed with people wearing black, the men with large wooden phalli, which they'd pointed enthusiastically at the women whilst singing crude, folkloric songs. Some had wrapped slices of lard around their carved phalli.

Now, by the dark of night, everyone wore white and carried candles whilst eulogizing the Lord. The priests were out in force. Tonight was the eve of San Giorgio. I'd been told by the drunks in the bar that this was a night when anything could happen. Watch out for the frustrated housewives, the young girls with hot thighs, they said. Tonight they were all wild, all the women!

Every man had to go out and be ready for the approach of his very own Pagan Queen. Many children were born nine months after San Giorgio, or at least that was what the wooden-phalli-guys told me, big grins on their faces.

At this precise moment I was standing under an awning outside a bar overlooking the main piazza. There was a marble fountain in the middle, filled with dry leaves and cobwebs. I looked up and saw Gradisca standing there, all dressed in white, her face terribly pale. I realized with a jolt that she was not happy. Across a sea of faces our eyes met; then we looked away, as if by magnetic resistance.

Could I possibly be mistaken? This woman looked too pale, and her hair was too short, too dark. Wasn't this in fact Gradisca's sister, the woman I knew from the ice cream bar?

Again and again I felt my eyes involuntarily sliding back, dwelling on her.

If I could have stepped forward and put my hand on Gradisca's arm, the fantasy would have been dispelled. On the night of San Giorgio I would have overcome this thing that was consuming me.

Once or twice she threw a speculative glance in my direction, as if waiting for me, but somehow I couldn't bridge the gap. All I could manage was to torpidly follow her as she moved off, disappearing into a crowd assembled before a stage, where a skimpily dressed dancer was performing a sort of erotic Egyptian dance, as if to goad her audience to orgiastic feats.

I stood there, searching for Gradisca. Could she really be this pale virgin I had seen? Gradisca was a gold-burnished creature in a blood-red skirt. All summer I had watched her long hair cascading in auburn luxuriance down her tapered back.

It was winter now. In some mysterious way she had redefined herself—put herself beyond my reach.

When the dance was over I walked back to my house and let myself in, waiting as the slow-starting fluorescent tube threw a white glare over everything. On the floor in the hall, a stray dog I had adopted stood up and put her tail between her legs. I stroked her and told her to stay in her basket. She licked my hand gratefully.

With heavy steps I climbed the stairs and got into my cold, damp bed.

iv) Epilogue

Somewhere inside of me there's a little dark man, or maybe a large dark man.

Either way, he's dark, and darksome. He feels something has been lost which will never again be found. In fact it is *love* that has gone; for the rest of his days he must go in search of it; even though it will never again be there, perfect and wholly possessed, in his hands.

This evening I walked through my town. The clouds were flying fast. The mistral came blowing in, and a sheet of light sea-mist slid over the top of the valley. The shops were lit, and on the rim of the horizon a dark halo seemed to be rising from the choppy sea, although the spume was almost luminous as the breakers came hissing in.

In the watch shop I saw a Greek chorus of women, all doe-eyed and intent on me as I glanced inside to catch a glimpse of Gradisca. She was wearing her dark blue jeans that show off her slightly disproportionate rump, offset by her shapely legs.

Gradisca was standing in an almost choreographed position, twisting at the waist to look out of the plate glass window, her legs like vines encircling a pillar.

The women knew I had come to look at her. I could hear their chorus chanting as I passed:

"Who is that sad, prowling man, and why does he make no attempt to come in? Why does he always walk past without waving at us, greeting us? Why does he look at us but never come in and have words with us? Does he think we are stones? See the darkling thrush, see those melancholy eyes! Beware, beware, for he has drunk from melancholic springs and courted fair Persephone!"

As I walked away I felt a deep sadness, as if something were dying inside of me.

Even so I doubled back and hovered round the piazza that

Gradisca sometimes crosses on her way to and from the shop.

Driving rain whipped across the paving stones. The place was deserted. I waited under a palm tree, then decided to buy some red wine and steak and head back home.

At a corner of the piazza I crashed into Gradisca, in her raincoat and umbrella.

"Ciao," she said breezily, as if I were no one in particular.

As she crossed the street and headed for the river, a late sun broke through the clouds. There was something almost heroic about her slight figure, clutching her shopping bags and rushing homeward under the swaying palms, through squalls of illuminated rain.

I had spent all this time dreaming about her, observing her. Now that I had seen her subsumed at last—looking to all intents and purposes like any other human being—I was left with a question in my mind, a question I might never be able to answer.

Who the hell was she?

Have You Met Lumpa?

When Susan opened the door she looked utterly unchanged, still wearing that air hostess uniform after all those years: a blue cotton/polyester skirt to her knees; black indistinct shoes with low heels; a white silk blouse; and a splash of Hermés scarf in case anyone should be so bold as to glance at her tubular white throat.

Also: that trademark smile, dazzling, slightly insincere.

"Robert, where have you been? Haven't seen you for an absolute age! Come in!" She led me into her nondescript suburban Cambridge home, and I followed her down an intestinal corridor. "Earl Grey or Darjeeling?" she called out over her shoulder, on her way into the kitchen.

"I don't suppose you have any of the non-smoked variety?"

"Ha! Now sit down and tell me everything." Returning, she sank into a sofa, from which she surveyed me, crossing her hands in her lap. "Are you still keeping up with Jane?"

"Jane? Who's Jane?"

"Jane. That girl doing philosophy, the one who lisped. I thought she was lovely."

"Susan, that was twenty years ago."

"Well some people do stay in touch, you know."

"Jane is living in Rotterdam. Married to an optician, I think."

"Sounds boring, the way you put it." She wrinkled her nose, smiled. "Mind you, who am I to say anything? I live in a bungalow. I never imagined for one moment I would end up in a bungalow. Robert, I'm your classic spinster, although I still get men sniffing at me. I do everything you'd expect me to, and of course I'm far too middle class not to play bridge." She stood up. "Now what about that tea? Or would you prefer something stronger?"

"I could have a gin."

"Of course you could, Robert. Gin is one of life's little survival kits."

She walked over to a sideboard and mixed me a drink, adding a couple of ice-cubes. "What about your wife, what happened to her?"

"You know about my wife?"

"Robert, I know absolutely everything. It's because I'm a letter-writer."

"So you'll know she left me, then. Or I left her."

"People are terribly vague, aren't they?"

"I suppose I made myself impossible. So she walked out on me while I was abroad. By the time I got back she'd already gone, taking most of the furniture. Made one feel it was a different house. No towels. Dust everywhere. Mattress on the floor. I grew to bloody hate London, I really did. That's when I moved to the Languedoc."

"Dear Robert must be the only person in the world who hated living in a nice comfortable Georgian house in London."

"Oh I can assure you many people hate London, but it's not

actually London they hate at all."

"What do they hate, Robert?" She laughed with that plaintive crystal sound of hers, like someone about to burst into tears. "Oh this is just like university! You haven't changed a bit."

"They hate themselves, Susan. People hate themselves, but they blame it on everyone else." I stopped, and looked at her. "You seem quite happy. Content, really."

"Oh I am. I love my life, small as it is, unimportant, all my dreams gone up in smoke. Dreams are enemies that come to us in our youth."

I let that grand statement hang in the air, after considering it from all angles.

In the corner of my eye I sensed a movement at floor level. A kind of wobbling, lolloping motion. And then I saw it: A square, grey jellified lump propelling itself over the carpet, about the size of a small dog. It moved towards us, taking about a minute to cross the floor.

"Have you met Lumpa?" Susan asked. "My Japanese pet."

"What is it?"

"He's a kind of amoeba. A single-cell organism, they call it, which is rather a rude way of describing a living thing. I mean, we don't refer to humans as bipeds, do we?"

"It doesn't speak Japanese, I take it?"

"Don't be silly. How would I communicate with it if it spoke Japanese?" She laughed. "I just mean it was invented in Japan."

"Do you take it for walks?"

"Don't be ridiculous! Lumpa would hate that. Lumpa likes to lounge around the house with me, watching television and reading books. Don't you Lumpa?"

By now the thing had reached her legs, and was more or less wobbling against her ankles. Susan reached down and stroked its smooth skin. It trembled slightly when it sensed human contact. "This is the only thing that's ever loved me," she added. "And that includes you, Robert. Most men don't like cuddling. You know that, being one yourself. In fact they'd rather not see you at all, unless they've got nookie on their minds."

I looked away to avoid something pointed in her stare. Surely she did not think I had come for that?

Susan had obviously grown a bit strange in her isolation. Then, when I thought about it, I realized she'd always been strange. Before I could think of anything to say, she stood up. "I think it's time for your lunch, isn't it?"

I was overcome by dread at the thought of some ghastly comfort food lurking in her oven, and I was just about to open my mouth to signal that I had already eaten, when she disappeared into the kitchen and returned with a bowl and a whisk. She cracked two eggs into some milk, then whisked the mixture.

Lumpa had already begun moving towards me, the next available source of warmth. Thankfully once it sensed her coming back it stopped and lolloped back to her.

She patted it. "They're very easy to feed, far easier than dogs or cats. They're much more human, somehow; plus, no hair on the carpet."

I gave the wobbly thing a sceptical look. "What's human about it?"

"Now he's going to have his dinner, aren't you, Lumpa?" said Susan. "I love his warm skin. He's very sensual, you know, considering he reproduces by splitting himself in two. That means he doesn't even have a thingy."

She stroked its back and then, once it was practically vibrating with pleasure, poured the contents of the bowl into a little depression she had made in its back or stomach or head, whatever the case was. Lumpa, as I will condescend to call it, seemed to be savoring the egg mixture, which it absorbed like a sponge.

Susan dipped her finger into her gin and tonic, and ran it across Lumpa's back.

"Today there's a treat," she said, "Because Robert's come to see us after all these years."

We sat in silence for a while. I was puzzled, never having seen a large amoeba before, and also repulsed by the whole thing: a lonely woman lavishing her thwarted love on a single-cell pet, watched by a lover of old come to revisit what he knew twenty years ago.

As if reading my mind, she continued. "Some people can't stand him. Many of my friends think I've gone absolutely potty."

"Really?"

"Yes, and you do too, Robert. Don't be so bloody devious. You were always devious, and nothing's changed, has it?"

"Why do you call it Lumpa?"

"Because that's what it said on the packet. When he arrived in the post he was in a dormant state, he only started moving around once he was fed."

I sat listening for a long while without interrupting her. In fact, I watched her with growing alarm, much as one does a mental patient in a hospital, wondering how much further she would go. Would there be an end to the madness, or was it infinite? This was just how she used to be while we lay postprandial and post-coital in her bed in the hall of residence at university. In those days I had listened with half a mind.

"When those dreadful people flew the planes into the World Trade Center," she began, "Lumpa would have survived. He'd have been fine. He would have jumped out of the window, and when he hit the ground he would have been smashed into hundreds of little pieces. But every little piece would crawl off and start a new life, every little piece of Lumpa would still be Lumpa, every piece would grow and then divide and sub-divide, because Lumpa can't be extinguished. He has a great zest for life. He is always the same, absolutely content. He wobbles along like a dear little thing. He's not exactly handsome but he doesn't mind. He's never in a bad mood, always affectionate."

The image of Lumpa in a thousand pieces on a Manhattan sidewalk was pathetic. I shifted uncomfortably in my chair.

To cap it all, Susan unscrewed the lid from a jar of Marmite and spread some of the foul-smelling paste over Lumpa's back.

Lumpa shivered and seemed to savor the goodness of B12.

"Now wait there," said Susan. "Digest while I rustle up some lunch for Robert."

Before I could say anything she had gone into the kitchen to wash her hands, returning with plates and cutlery. I could see her opening the oven where she was harboring what looked like a mushroom omelette. While she was bustling about in there, I examined Lumpa in more detail. On a conceptual level, I found its being deeply offensive, the way it would have crawled quite happily to anyone, possibly even a serial killer or wife-beater, giving to each its very own unconditional love. Even on a microcosmic level there was something disgusting about little tiny cells of Lumpa wobbling about in search of sustenance.

On an analytical level, I realized this was the very basis of all life on earth. The very air we breathed was full of minute Lumpas, all pursuing their meaningless lives without any awareness of their purpose.

I forced myself to touch Lumpa. Its skin was warm, quite dry, almost like human skin.

As soon as Lumpa felt my touch, it started vibrating and I fancied I could make out some strange throbbing sounds from its jellified body.

I pulled my hand away, but Lumpa was not content. Lumpa started coming for me. There was something absolutely irrepressible about its movement, and I realized that wherever I went in the world, Lumpa would always be following me like a heat-seeking blob. Whenever I slept, I would wake up to find it nestling against my body.

Susan called out from the kitchen. "Do you want cheese on your omelette?"

Her question was like an accusation. She must have known that I wanted nothing less than a cheese and mushroom omelette.

"No thanks, Susan! No cheese!"

I picked up a little fork from my tea-tray and with all my might drove it up to the hilt into Lumpa's body. For a moment it stopped moving and seemed to shiver with discomfort, then redoubled its efforts to get even closer to me, in a soft, warm place where nothing could hurt it.

The fork stuck out of its back like an absurd mast. There was no blood, of course, just a tiny bit of ooze.

I stood up and very quietly tiptoed down the carpeted corridor to the front door, which clicked too noisily behind me.

Keeping an eye over my shoulder, I walked smartly back to my car.

Little Rabbit

Back in those days, I wasn't sleeping so well. I kept having dreams about being a criminal on trial. In the dreams, it was a stifling hot summer somewhere in Central Europe. I sat beside my lawyer through interminable afternoons, listening to the shuffling and fidgeting of the spectators behind me. Overhead, the high windows let in a stream of filtered sunlight, palely reflecting the brilliance of its source.

Once awake, I made notes in my dream diary:

"The judge is in his early sixties, a stern and judicious presence with silver temples. His hard voice rings out, and as I listen to his ranting speeches globules of his spit arc wildly across the courtroom..."

My therapist said I had melodramatic tendencies, although she assured me this was quite normal. At night I'd lie there in my bed, wondering at my transformation into a malcontent. Where was that well-adjusted young man I used to be, the graduate with his loafers, his navy blue sweater, his straightforward willingness to discuss Keats's letters?

A Brazilian samba-bard wrote in one of his songs: *"I am not navigating the sea, the sea is navigating me."* This seemed to touch on some pertinent truth, as a vast ocean beyond my understanding had entered my body, leaving me gasping.

One day I woke up and things snapped into place, snapped into place and fell apart like a rotten fruit.

Until recently, I'd been living a fairly satisfactory life. Like most of my friends I considered myself a potential film director or, failing that, an installation artist or multimedia specialist. I spent a lot of my time sitting around in cafés discussing films and exhibitions, or filling in forms, grant applications and such like. I lived in a fantastic apartment in Belsize Park, London, on a street where Tim Burton and Helena Bonham-Carter were often seen, he wearing his weird pink airman's goggles, she like a bony, sexy witch wrapped up in a feather boa. I used to have fantasies of going up to Tim and telling him about one of my projects, director to director so to speak, but of course I had never directed a film.

In those days I was always planning my next move, trying to figure out how to shin up the greasy old pole. At the beginning of May each year, regular as a migrating grey-lag goose, I'd pack my suitcase and head off to Cannes Film Festival for another round of taunts and ritual humiliation devised by fatter and more devious men or sharp-heeled castrators.

My efforts seemed to count for nothing, none of my feature film scripts had ever gone into production. Most of my disposable income was spent on coffee and snacks in a local Soho café where a whole bunch of fledgling screenwriters liked to sit with their laptops, thoughtfully scratching their immature beards while knocking up the latest magnum opus and waiting for Tim Burton to walk past. But what were we all *really* waiting for?—that's the question I ask myself now.

That famous *oasis* we yearned for—the one where Warren Beatty and Julie Christie sat conversing pleasantly on one's Malibu terrace, as one emerged firing witty, semi-automatic wise-cracks—was really *a desert.* It was a euphemism for a large, comfortable house in Hampstead Heath full of kitchen machines and haunted by a frustrated woman with large haunches who seemed to spend most of her time either trying not to eat cake or wishing we'd go out for dinner more often. The prospect of divorce hung over the whole scenario like a vulture.

Each morning, as one opened one's eyes and heard Julie Christie cackling out there on the terrace while Warren lit his sixty-third cigarette, it grew clearer that nothing but ambition had led one here. The substantive nightmare was composed of fantasy.

For that reason I had chosen to remain single though I was thirty-six. A snide friend of mine by name of Clarissa taunted me once that I did not want a real woman with warts and blemishes, I wanted a Barbie doll that was alive. Which was not strictly true. I don't find Barbie very attractive. Her hips are non-existent and she's sickeningly neurotic with all her accessories. Imagine the hours by the mirror before she'd leave the house, scarcely able to walk in her pin-cushion shoes? If you asked Barbie who Krishnamurti was, she'd probably very sweetly tell you he was a Bengali corn-snack or possibly a lesser actor with a walk-on part in a Bollywood musical.

Women, for the most part, were in the mud-bath with the rest of us, grappling and kicking and farting in the slime while crowds of barbarians stood roaring and heckling and clapping. Women read erudite books on their sexuality, invented whole creeds of female empowerment which centered on the sacred right of twiddling the nether parts of whomsoever they liked. Then of course there were the diagrams of the topography of one's genitalia in the glossy self-help manuals: *If you press here, you will feel a pleasant sensation. Slide your finger over this thing, and an immediate gushing orgasm will surprise you greatly.*

In my home there was no food bubbling in the cooking pots, no irate thirty-something woman eating celery and spending hours on the treadmill, no teeming children rampaging through the house, throwing water-balloons at each other and short-circuiting the television.

And now we come to the operative point. In my diaries, all packed up now and kept in a locked suitcase under the sofa, I had some poems I wrote about a fictitious daughter named Little Rabbit. When Little Rabbit came along, she would change my world. With her radiance and energy she would transform the universe and, like a bright beam of love, be the flame under the morning kettle, the key in the ignition, the electrical current in the fan keeping me cool through the summers. Little Rabbit would march into my existence in the manner of the Red Army entering Warsaw, looting the art museum and aiming bazookas at the Cabinet Office with its hushed corridors and waxed floors.

In my poem, I wrote, "Little Rabbit, you are not very polite,/ But in your way you will redeem/ Each thing I ever felt..."

And this was where I always got stuck, when I was with my shrink. You see, I felt it was wrong expecting some poor little kid to redeem an eternal child like me. My shrink disagreed. She told me these types of hopes were metaphorical on the whole, a way of structuring reality to make it palatable to the suffering individual. Furthermore, when you're wiping your baby's arse at four in the morning, it's important to bear in mind that this screaming and obnoxious little thing is actually your redemption.

She also explained that people tended to see themselves in a dramatic sense, as figures on a fresco or perhaps an Etruscan vase. Running, reaching, singing, playing a dulcimer, or kissing. Love is that moment when the figure on the urn suddenly breaks through the void and catches up with the supreme immortal runner whose sinewy legs confidently scale mountains; the moment when the protagonist supersedes humanity, outpacing divinity for an instant and *snatching the bunch of golden grapes* out of the hands of the outraged god; then, bare feet drumming against the warm sandy earth, slowing down and coming to rest in a grove somewhere at the edge of the world where a woman waits, a woman with dark moist eyes.

After this victory comes the life of repose, the earned stillness, the sacred fire burning in the evenings, the meat dripping with fat, the fragrance of olive leaves crackling as they burn, and from that time the children start coming forth like a sort of ultimate harvest, perfectly made like tiny Swiss watches, all the parts spinning and turning and whirring and ticking.

Having got me thus far, my shrink ruined the whole thing by suggesting I was a reincarnation of an ancient Greek man, my head thus filled with classical musings. It appealed to my vanity, you see. The feeding and nurturing of the ego is all very well, but I didn't want to console myself by feeling I was some great and profound guy who once lived and buggered in Athens where he wrote poetry and practiced the discus in his spare time—whereas, in actual fact, I was a mid-thirties aspiring film director who never did much except play squash twice a week and drink a hell of a lot of cappuccino.

This was the state of play for me, until a certain telephone call.

When I picked up, I was actually in the midst of devising a denouement to my fantasy thriller. I modulated my voice, adding a note of barely restrained irritation as I answered, just in case the person at the other end of the line imagined that her telephone call was a welcome distraction. I had already seen from the telephone display that the caller was none other than Clarissa, famous in our circles for organizing tea parties in honor of some personage or other she's picked up—usually a Mongolian painter, Georgian nose-flute player or Etruscan chiropodist—tea parties where you have to eat weird locust biscuits from Eritrea washed down with goat-juice while conversing with a Bengali poet and taxi driver.

"John, I'm not disturbing your creative flow, am I? If I am, just tell me." Clarissa always begins by apologizing herself off the planet, forcing you to interrupt, be rude and put yourself at a disadvantage.

"Yes I *was* working on the script actually," I said with a tired sigh. "But don't worry. I'm not *really* working."

"Oh dear! Are you all right?"

"Clarissa." I ground my teeth until I remembered the dentist had told me not to. "What do you want?"

"You know my friend from St. Petersburg?"

"Who?"

"I introduced you, don't you remember? I promised to put her up when she had her audition at the Royal College of Music, but she just called now and she's flying in tomorrow which is an utter pain because I've got that Indonesian family coming. From Singapore. You know, the sushi chef and his wife who makes shadow-puppets?"

"What's all this got to do with me?"

Clarissa sighed, then launched into a brilliant pitch, so brilliant that I found myself wondering why the hell she wasn't working in the film industry. "It has everything to do with you, John, we're all connected, not separate like you think... I can't fit them all in! Oh John, please! She's only a tiny little Russian girl from St. Petersburg, absolutely sweet, only twenty-one. You can boss her about as much as you like, she won't be difficult, and she's a musical prodigy, plays the piano like she invented the bloody thing. She had a grant from the Guggenheim Foundation, you know. Her family's penniless, her father lost a leg in a knife-fight and—"

"Her father lost his leg in a knife-fight? How the hell did he manage that?"

"She's staying for a week. Can you do it or not?"

"A week! Are you out of your mind!" I paused. "You know, I've been meaning to ask you something, Clarissa. In your view, is Krishnamurti a philosopher or a Bengali corn-snack?"

"John! Why do you always have to be such a prick? I'm asking you a small favor here. What's a week in the grand scheme of things?"

In the end I think it may have been the music angle that sealed it for me. I love music, it may even be the only thing I care about at all. I have an amazing piano that used to belong to my mother; I've been told it's a really excellent one, made in Leipzig with a solid dye-cast frame or something. It occurred to me that I'd love to hear Chopin's *Nocturnes* played on it.

When the doorbell rang the next day, I was caught off guard. I suppose I was expecting some tiny rotund Natasha in a shawl, barefoot, covered in head-lice and clutching a filthy cardboard box tied up with string.

I knew something was up as soon as I opened the door. Clarissa was standing there with her arms crossed, peering down her nose at me. The silly thing was wearing a knitted Peruvian poncho and long black button-up boots, and I had the oddest feeling—odd because I was convinced I was right—she was trying to tart herself up. But why? Clarissa was a battleship, knew she was a battleship. Even on cursory examination I saw the whelks of belly-fat spilling over the lining of her trousers. I felt sorry for her. I think there may even have been an owlish boyfriend somewhere in her life, or an ex-boyfriend secreted in some back bedroom. She certainly wasn't dressing for my benefit, and not for his either.

Then I saw the reason. That most primitive of feminine motivations.

Behind her stood Olga, and Olga was *very* pretty. She had long eyelashes, bright, mischievous eyes and high cheekbones like a Mongolian nomad.

Clarissa wrung her hands. "This is Olga. We haven't seen each other in three years. And here she is..." She turned round and waved her arms in the air, as if overwhelmed by her once-so-young protégé, who'd grown into this womanly creature all fragrant and dense with purpose, having wafted in on the Aeroflot iron bird and now standing unfurled before us.

"Hello, Olga." I reached out and shook her hand. When I spoke, I articulated as clearly as I could. "You. Are. Very. Welcome."

"Hello, John," she replied. "Very kind of you to have me." She had an attractive, fluid American accent, as if nurtured on a diet of Walt Whitman, Leo Tolstoy, and *Time* magazine. As I was turning round to lead them into the house I felt a wave of hostility from Clarissa catch me across the stern and almost capsize me in its towering waves. Suddenly I understood that I had been a prick for years. It had something to do with standing there opposite Clarissa in black button-up boots tight as sausage-skins around her bulging calves. Clarissa, with faint rouge brushed across her cheeks, feeling ignored and overlooked and burning with resentment, while I admired the younger woman.

I took Clarissa and Olga inside; proudly I led them across my kitchen with the newly fitted floor of hand-made Spanish terracotta tiles, the under-floor heating which had cost me the equivalent of a two-year supply of cappuccinos. Nick Cave would have a floor just like mine, I was sure of it. Anyone cool would have a floor just like that. They'd keep it mopped and clean at all times, so that early in the morning with a nice frothy cafe latte and the iBook open and the wireless running, they could cross the shining floor in bare feet or maybe a pair of *havaianas* and carelessly knock up a few sonnets prior to the goddess calling out from the bedroom for croissants and coconut milk.

As I stopped to let them pass in front of me into the sitting room, I noticed that Olga had an ample body without any of that unpleasant stoutness I associate with child-bearing. She was wearing black corduroys, fairly tight, with a woven belt. Her face had a beautiful light bronzed tone, and I had no trouble imagining a gold stud in her nostril and a necklace of unpolished Yemeni turquoise tucked into her generously swelling cleavage.

No doubt about it, Clarissa was out of her comfort zone. She brought her large posterior down in the sofa with a severe jolt, like a tree falling in a forest. The role of the *madam* was deeply irksome to her: delivering this ingénue free-of-charge to me, a person for whom she had little respect. I sensed her unsettled mind, its dark gyroscope spinning at enormous speed, trying to work its way out of this unbearable situation, whilst balancing on a pin-head above the void.

While I was in the kitchen making a pot of green tea, I heard Clarissa's theatrical whispers from next-door. "I'm sorry about this, Olga. If you don't like it here I can probably fit you into my box room if you'd prefer."

Then the perfectly modulated American voice of Olga, vaguely amused but also respectful. She really did pack a punch. "No, really Clarissa, it's fine for me. I am very happy."

"You're sure now? It's no trouble. He's not as bad as he seems."

"He seems very nice."

I came back in with the tea-tray, on which I had also put some sesame and honey biscuits bound to appeal to Clarissa. We sat in silence for a few moments, listening to the sound of the gas-flames from my remote-controlled imitation log-fire. When you consider my spectacular lack of success in the movie industry, it was no mean achievement, all the various signals I'd invested the room with. Apart from the obligatory ruinous electronics, I'd had a bookshelf built along the main wall filled with complicated-sounding titles, most of which I'm keeping for later, when I have more time: *The Rustle of Language*, *The Use of Pleasure*, *Regarding the Pain of Others*, *Illness as Metaphor*, *The Archaeology of the Frivolous*, *The Ear of the Other*, *In Defence of Lost Causes*, *In Search of Wagner*, and so on.

Olga tasted a biscuit, then, after chewing thoughtfully, said, "John, if you and Clarissa are hungry, I could make some lunch for us. I did some shopping earlier and I brought some things from Russia. I didn't want to arrive empty-handed."

Clarissa laughed and slapped her thigh playfully. "Oh you shouldn't spoil John, he hasn't had lunch at home for years, he just goes out and has an old cheese sandwich or something!"

"Poor guy!" said Olga and chuckled. Her voice had a crystal-clear undertone but no shrillness, like a murmuring bell from across a valley. She stood up and went to some luggage she'd left by the door. After rummaging for a while, she disappeared and we heard the sounds of chopping, frying, and stirring from the kitchen.

I looked at Clarissa and made sure I sounded as irritated as possible: "Everything all right, pet? Time of the month, is it?"

Clarissa wasn't buying it. "Just take it easy, John. She's twenty-one, for Christ's sake. I thought you were a grown man!"

"What the hell are you talking about?"

"Whatever," she muttered. "It's my fault. I brought her here. I shouldn't have."

"What do you think I'm going to do, eat her?"

"I'm sure you'd like to!"

"You're unfair, Clarissa. I'm doing you a favor and suddenly it's like I'm doing something wrong."

"Your eyes are on stalks, John!"

Having nothing else to say, we strayed into the kitchen, where Olga was making a pie. She'd gutted and filleted several large mackerel and layered them with breadcrumbs and onions pre-fried in a deep slick of butter. Over the top she tossed a sheet of yellow, buttery pastry, which she expertly fixed to the sides of the oven-tray with deft, rapid finger movements.

Clarissa hiccupped when she saw all that saturated fat in the frying pan. "Wow, you like butter, don't you? I don't know how you keep your figure!"

For the first time Olga lost a little of her composure. She swung round. "Butter is good for you! Everyone knows that.

Keeps you regular, too."

"Who told you that?" Clarissa said. "Your mum?"

"Actually my mother's dead."

"I'm sorry, I didn't mean to… I'm a little stressed out." Her voice sounded brittle. She swayed a little and held on to my granite work-top. I patted her on the shoulder. "Why don't you lay the table, Clarissa? I'll help Olga here."

By now, Olga was transferring the contents of one of her large hold-alls to my freezer and refrigerator. First there were countless tins of salmon caviar, jars of potted wild mushrooms, oozing parcels of smoked sausage, hard-boiled quail's eggs. Then, clinking like loaded weapons as she unwrapped them, bottle after bottle of herb vodka wrapped in damp newspaper. That's the sort of thing I like: a house-guest who, without a word, stuffs your freezer with vodka.

Olga's preparations were made efficiently and calmly, her face in deep concentration as she asked where I kept candlesticks and cutlery. When I showed her, she frowned. "It's a shame for brass candlesticks to be full of green stains like this, John. I will polish them for you."

"You really don't need to."

"But I want to." Her eyes were sober, dark and bursting with purpose.

"What about your piano practice? Do you really have time for that?"

"I have time for everything. This is nice cutlery. It's old silver and you shouldn't keep it all together like this. It'll get scratched."

Next door, Clarissa was dabbing her eyes with a tissue. I put my arm round her larded waist. "It's okay, Clarissa, let's have a nice lunch now and relax." She somewhat frenetically apologized and then hyperventilated about the Indonesians coming later, how her flat was in a real mess and she hadn't done any shopping and her overdraft at the bank had been cancelled so she didn't have any money.

It seemed too good an opportunity to miss, in terms of getting old misery guts off my neck and laying a guilt trip on her, which might just shut her up for a while. Quickly I flashed her a generous smile and offered her a cash loan, making sure I was counting out a bunch of fifty-pound notes just as Olga peered in. When she registered I was giving Clarissa money, her smile deepened, as if she now considered me a man of substance, a kind, considerate man, which I'm not. But she also could not resist a little joke. "How much did he pay you for me?" she asked Clarissa, who burst into a shrill laugh, sounding like a banshee getting ready to slit her own throat.

There was a moment of silence resettling itself, then Olga said, in a composed and pleasant voice: "Lunch will be ready in about twenty minutes. Anyone for a drink?"

I was starting to feel rather heavenly. I leaned back in the sofa as Olga brought in a tray of savory biscuits and bowls of Lord-knows-what, sort of yogurt with cucumber and smoked fish, feta cheese with fruit or something. It tasted great with cold white Georgian wine.

Clarissa was not quite herself for the rest of the lunch. She left all tangled up in apologies, after helping us put the dirty crockery away in the dishwasher. I only just managed to resist the urge of poking my tongue at her. As soon as the door closed, Olga breathed a sigh of relief. She picked up her bags and went to her room, where for about twenty minutes I heard her opening and closing drawers, taking hangers from the wardrobe and carefully putting away her dresses. "John, do you have an iron?" she called out.

"What? An iron?" I closed my eyes, tried to remember where I'd put the damned thing, then fetched it for her.

I couldn't help but stand there watching as she ironed a blouse with fierce attention. When she finished, she looked at me with a shy, yet also delighted, smile. "You know if I see a wrinkled blouse it sort of makes my head spin," she said. "And now I'm going to polish your brass. I have to do something to be useful for you."

"You really don't have to."

"Don't be polite. It makes everything so silly," she said, then spread newspapers across my kitchen table. After disappearing into her bedroom and changing into a pair of scuffed-up jeans and a T-shirt, she got on with rubbing the life out of not only my candle-sticks but also my copper-plated cooking pots and anything else she could find round the flat.

It took bloody hours. When she was finishing, she looked at me. "Do you have silver polish?"

"What?"

"Silver polish. Do you have silver polish? For your cutlery?"

"No, no, it's fine! You don't have to polish it, Olga!"

"I'm going to polish your silver!" Her eyes expanded, and her mouth tensed. "I can't stand seeing beautiful things like this, not cared for."

It was true, but who gives a damn about some old knives and forks? My grandmother had given me a box full of them. Solid, ornate silver from the early eighteen hundreds, probably valuable, should have sold them years ago. "So I'll go and get some silver polish," I finally said.

"Thank you."

The supermarket was round the corner, so I was only gone for ten minutes or so, but as soon as I opened the front door I heard the piano. She was a prodigy all right. I don't know what she was playing, but it sounded absolutely fantastic. The music saturated every molecule in my flat, the energy cleaning everything. I stood in the doorway like a speck of dust fighting a current of fresh air.

When she paused, I closed the door and walked in. She was startled. "You don't mind me playing your piano, do you?"

"Mind?" I shook my head. "I love it. Please play it whenever you like. In fact I order you to play it! Don't worry about disturbing me. I'm one of those weird people who only work in cafés. Mainly I just hang about and drink coffee and end up running into some loser and having an argument about the Coen brothers."

Surreptitiously I put down the tube of silver polish, but she noticed straight away and determinedly shut the lid of the piano. "Good, you got the polish."

"No, no! I want you to keep playing."

She smiled and shook her head. "First I polish, then I play. John, I can't play if things aren't right, do you understand?"

It was revolutionary, to me, the whole concept of *things needing to be right*. It didn't conform with the sort of view of the universe I'd built up over the years.

"What do you think of my piano?"

She caressed its black-shining flank, its gold-embossed letters. "I like it very much, but it needs tuning." A little wrinkle played across her pale forehead, then, with great hesitation, she said: "If I pay for it, John, can we have it tuned?"

"But I had it tuned!"

"When?"

I ran my hand through my hair, trying to think. "Oh, about ten years ago."

"Ten years ago?" She smiled, and put her hand on my arm. "You see? So it needs another tune."

Once again I found myself in full retreat, like a splash of rancid milk running across a skewed floor. Finally, after much swallowing, I agreed. "Okay, you can have it tuned, but I will pay for it."

"No, John, I will pay."

"I said, I will pay!"

It was silly, really, the stand-off. She shrugged and didn't say anything else, except that she knew someone in London who was a piano-tuner, and she'd give him a call.

A few hours later, coming home from the café, I was surprised to find a bearded and dandruff-spattered Russian with a spectacularly receding hairline already at work on the piano. Olga was sitting cross-legged in the sofa, like a lit candle, reading intently from a book. She closed it with a snap.

"Was I too fast?" she asked.

"Fast? No..."

"I just thought, why not take care of the problem?"

"That's an angle, I guess." I stuck a finger into my ear and started digging around, as if ear-wax might relieve my discomfort.

"I thought you'd be out working all day."

I leaned back in the sofa and stared vacantly at the ceiling. "Olga, have you ever tried working all day in a café? It's bloody impossible."

She laughed. "Of course it is. Why don't you stay here in your great apartment? All that money you're wasting on coffee, John, you could buy the best Arabica beans and sit in your garden and get a lot done. Right?"

Before I knew it, Olga had paid the guy and was shaking his hand. As soon as he'd gone, she started practicing in earnest. She played for about an hour, filling the house with the same sequences played over and over again almost mechanically. It worried me. Scenes are never good if you rewrite them too many times.

I spent a few largely unproductive hours under the chestnut tree in the garden, sipping at some good strong Arabica coffee, as she'd advised. It seemed largely redundant, trying to flesh out the details of the ending of my fantasy thriller, the one where my main character learns that his body is diseased and filled with maggots.

I knew in my heart the film would never be made.

The wind ruffled the swaying crown of the horse-chestnut tree, and I concentrated on the sound of the piano being played inside, the harmonizing notes and scales. It stopped and the piano stool scraped against the floor. Olga stuck her head out of the garden door. "John, do you want to come for a walk?"

The first week passed in the wink of an eye, and before I knew it, one had turned into two, then three.

We'd get up and have a silent breakfast, usually with eggs and coffee and toast dripping with melted butter. I have a weird tendency to eat things like Stilton and avocado first thing in the morning, but Olga never commented. In fact she seemed utterly unconcerned, which I appreciated.

One thing she did in the mornings was to practice the piano on the table. Her fingers moved about, as if there was a keyboard there. Obviously there was no sound.

I decided I would not comment on her habits, just as she didn't comment on mine.

There was a friendly, plausible atmosphere of mutual respect between us.

Sometimes Olga brought out a coffee into the garden where I was working. If I ever dared give her a compliment she'd reply ironically, like a sort of Winona Ryder character, then walk back inside slightly pissed with me. Another great thing about Olga was she loved fish fingers and Heinz baked beans. We took it in turn to shove the sods under the grille and eat them without any fuss. It saved a lot of cooking time. If one is unlucky enough to be alive in the twenty-first century, one might as well make the most of its conveniences.

Lunch was also usually silent, and I heartily approved of this. I can't imagine Warren and Julie did much blabbering while he was figuring out the *Shampoo* storyline and doing his best to control Robert Towne's excesses. I reckon Warren and Julie must have had a lot of intense, silent fucking, but apart from that they were probably just working their balls off.

Me and Olga, on the other hand, had a strange reluctance to cross into the land of the lucky. Occasionally we'd playfully entwine our fingers as we walked along, but that was it. I liked the way her steps more or less kept time with mine, so that sometimes we were like two soldiers marching along.

For the time being I was saving a fortune by my boycott of cappuccinos and ciabatta rolls, and this was good enough for me.

A few times when we had sunny days we climbed to the top of Primrose Hill and looked out over London from that spot where the gallows had once stood. Once people were strung up there, but now it's a well-known meeting-place for lovers, who sit huddled together, admiring the sun going down over the city.

One evening the sun was making a masterpiece of the industrial smog suspended over Wembley to the west, and Olga sat there humming a sequence of notes from the Bartok number she was learning for the audition whilst practicing a complex sequence of finger movements in the grass. Without thinking too much about it I leaned forward and gave her a resounding kiss on the lips.

"What was that for?" she said, without taking her eyes off the grass.

"I just felt I should."

The air between us was pregnant after that. When we got back to the flat, Olga disappeared into her room for a moment to change into a black, sheer dress and tied her hair back. There was a sort of vitality about her, like a bright green papaya tree rising out of the undergrowth.

She went into the kitchen to knock up a pudding, explaining that she needed some sugar. Without a word she handed me a plate of figs with flamed ginger, toasted *panetone,* and home-made vanilla sauce, possibly the most delicious thing I had ever eaten.

I ate, then broke the silence: "Olga, is there anything you can't do?"

"There are two things I can't do," she replied in a no-nonsense voice. "I can't play the piano as well as I'd like. And I can't meet a man capable of loving me the way I want to be loved."

Her words issued from her mouth like a mist. In the end I decided to fill in the missing words myself. "If you fell in love with me, Olga, I think you'd be satisfied."

"I'm not so sure about that John. We all say things because they sound good, and we'd like them to be true."

She stared hard at me, and I nervously retreated. "I'm being hypothetical anyway."

"Hypothetical? I don't even know what that means, but it sounds like bullshit." She stood up and went to the bedroom, returning with her arms full of pillows, sheets and a duvet. These she arranged in front of the fire. I went and sat by her, then leaned forward and kissed her. She had a lovely, soft body. I had a feeling I shouldn't touch her, but I couldn't stop myself, nor did she stop me. Her breasts were very ripe for someone so young, and yet they had flattened slightly around the nipple as if once overfilled with milk and now ready to be filled again. Even this, the thought of her imminent pregnancy, enflamed me, and I had a sense that I would possess her womb fully and make her grow down there again and again, until we grew old and our children sat round us at the table.

At the base of her spine was a fleshy little fold of skin across the top of her buttocks. I ran my finger along it, imagining myself riding her.

Later, everything I had imagined happened exactly as I fantasized. It was as if I'd foreseen her gift for physical love. Whatever the soothsayers say about the dangers of physical attraction as a causal factor, I knew I was bound to her and powerless to resist, even if it meant dying, starving, being ripped to shreds between wild horses or cut into small pieces and lowered into boiling oil, then fed to wild pigs. My body impelled me, even as everything in the world warned me to beware of that message, that simple crude rallying call of her body lying stretched out before me like a landscape, a landscape in which I saw my children, and my grandchildren and great-grandchildren all laboring on the land, tilling it and brutalizing their oxen until the furrows were done, straight and narrow and filled with onion and beets and beans.

"Oh God, Olga, you make me so happy!" I groaned as I lunged into her and found her ready for me, in fact so wet that at first I was startled. When I put my finger in her mouth, she sucked on it so greedily that I thought I'd expire with joy, but then she brought the whole delight to a sort of purposeful resolution by declaring, in a vaguely amused tone, "Your fingers taste of garlic, John, when you wash them you must scrub your nails..." Which didn't stop her carrying on sucking my fingers. Her vulva seemed so custom-made for me that my every lunge into her body produced an exquisite exhalation of air.

Afterwards we lay still for a while, holding our breaths, too happy to speak.

"Have you made love many times before?" I said.

"I've had many fucks, but lately they haven't meant so very much to me."

Strangely enough I believed her implicitly. Indeed, it seemed inconceivable that she had ever made love to anyone except me. Just the thought of it made me itchy. When it got very late, we gathered up the bedclothes and went to bed, sleeping very deeply until the alarm went off at about six in the morning and she got up and made her preparations for her audition.

Before she left she came to me and said: "I'd like to know something before I go. Is this real? Will you still be here this evening?"

"I'll be here. I live here," I said.

"But I don't live here, do I? So the question is... what happens now?"

"Well, I'd like to see more of you," I said ineptly. My words had a kind of natural resistance. They rolled across my tongue traitorously, as if harboring little daggers and sub-contractual exemptions and clauses, all later to be expounded by lawyers and learned cynics.

She stood in the door for a long, long time, a tiny wrinkle between her eyebrows growing and growing until it covered her entire face. "The trouble is I think you have a lot of shit in you."

"I never said I didn't, did I Olga?"

"Does that make it any better?"

I propped myself up on one elbow, frowning and vaguely overwhelmed. "Can't we just take one day at a time?"

When she left the house, there was a finality to the way the door closed.

I threw on some clothes, opened the door and ran into the street to follow her, but I couldn't see her anywhere.

I waited all day in a growing fever of anticipation for her to come home.

As evening set in, my misgivings grew. I telephoned Clarissa, who knew nothing, although she found it difficult to mask her delight at the sense that something had gone wrong. She offered me a bitter pastille with relish. "John, I haven't heard from Olga for days, and I've been very busy myself. Maybe she met some students her own age at the college and went dancing. That's what twenty-one-year-olds do. Had you forgotten?"

Darkness descended. It was a darkness I recognized, because I had been living in it all my life until the day Olga arrived.

My nerves were playing havoc with me. I went out and bought a packet of cigarettes, then sat smoking in the garden under the chestnut tree, talking to myself and growing frenzied as I once again relived last night. It struck me that if I could not see Olga again I would be indifferent to everything in life from this day on. I would happily step into the void and fall, whilst quietly smoking a pipe or reflectively turning the pages of a volume of poems, occasionally quoting a line from it until my body hit the ground with an incandescent, star-colliding impact.

Midnight struck and I knew everything was doomed. I opened a half-bottle of Bell's and sat there smoking and drinking for hours, until I was suddenly overwhelmed by a violent fit of vomiting. Instinctively I knew that Olga was also vomiting somewhere at this very moment. I pined for her, I wanted to hold her and protect her.

Dawn broke.

Finally, at six in the morning, the key turned in the lock and Olga walked in. With a deep sigh that racked her whole body she sat down at the kitchen table, and stared gloomily at the floor.

"I failed my audition," she said. "So I walked all night. I walked into the East End and met some boys and went to a party with them. College boys. They'd hired a place with a live band, and they had ice sculptures and you could drink shots of vodka from the tits of the female sculptures and the penises of the male sculptures." She looked up, heartbroken. "I had many, many shots, John. Then I met a man who said he found me fascinating. He wanted to take me with him to India, leaving next week."

I stood looking at her, felt the color draining from my face.

"Then I started dancing, and the drink was bubbling in my body, and I felt wild. I took off most of my clothes and danced on the table. I kept vomiting until another man came to help me. He cleaned me up. He was handsome and he seemed interested in me."

She gazed at me.

"But I kept thinking I'd rather be with the man I knew." She stood up laboriously and sighed. "I'm going to take a shower and then let's sleep all day. Okay?"

"Okay."

I put my hand on her arm, feeling the urge to say something decisive, not only for her but also for myself. I struggled for a while, and then the words surfaced with great clarity. Later, examining those words, I felt they were my first ever work of art. "Don't worry, Olga. It will all turn out like a long summer's day…"

after tonight."

The others were entering the room now and Tarzan turned toward the little window.

But he saw nothing outside—within he saw a patch of greensward surrounded by a matted mass of gorgeous tropical plants and flowers, and, above, the waving foliage of mighty trees, and, over all, the blue of an equatorial sky.

In the center of the greensward a young woman sat upon a little mound of earth, and beside her sat a young giant. They ate pleasant fruit and looked into each other's eyes and smiled. They were very happy, and they were all alone.

His thoughts were broken in upon by the station agent who entered asking if there was a gentleman by the name of Tarzan in the party.

"I am Monsieur Tarzan," said the ape-man.

"Here is a message for you, forwarded from Baltimore; it is a cablegram from Paris."

Tarzan took the envelope and tore it open. The message was from D'Arnot.

It read:

Fingerprints prove you Greystoke. Congratulations.

D'ARNOT.

As Tarzan finished reading, Clayton entered and came toward him with extended hand.

Here was the man who had Tarzan's title, and Tarzan's estates, and was going to marry the woman whom Tarzan loved—the woman who loved Tarzan. A single word from Tarzan would make a great difference in this man's life.

It would take away his title and his lands and his castles, and—it would take them away from Jane Porter also. "I say, old man," cried Clayton, "I haven't had a chance to thank you for all you've done for us. It seems as though you had your hands full saving our lives in Africa and here.

"I'm awfully glad you came on here. We must get better acquainted. I often thought about you, you know, and the remarkable circumstances of your environment.

"If it's any of my business, how the devil did you ever get into that bally jungle?"

"I was born there," said Tarzan, quietly. "My mother was an Ape, and of course she couldn't tell me much about it. I never knew who my father was."

THE END